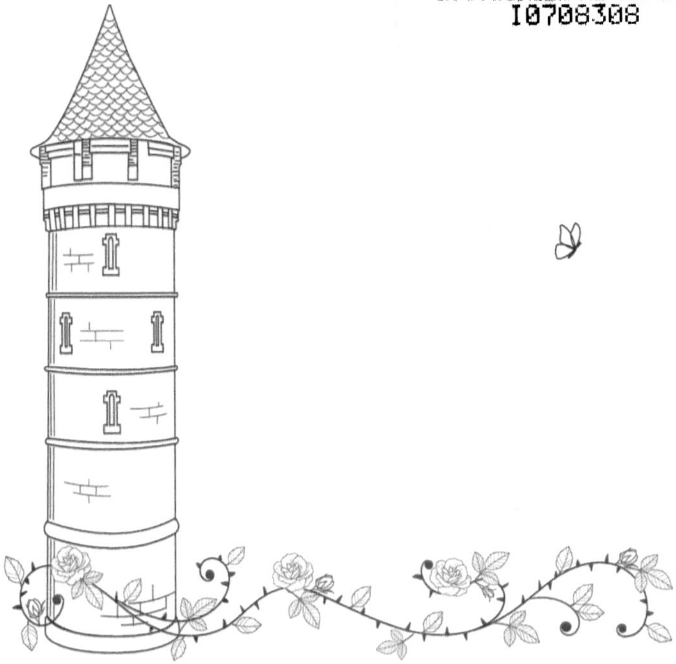

IMPOSSIBLE TASKS

Alexa Santi

Copyright © 2023 by Alexa Santi

Cover design by Enchanted Ink Studio © 2025

Illustrations by Magic Book Cover Design

All rights reserved.
No part of this book may be reproduced in any form or by any electronic or mechanical means, including information storage and retrieval systems, without written permission from the author, except for the use of brief quotations in a book review.

ISBN: 979-8-9896182-0-0

Contents

Chapter One

Lorien opened his eyes as soon as the footsteps of his captors faded away. He tested his fetters first—iron, of course, not only on his wrists and ankles, but around his throat as well. They were taking no chances with his magic.

He spared a moment to tamp down the rage that threatened to bubble over. This situation required stealth and diplomacy, not the breaking of heads his father and brother would resort to. Brute force would not help him and likely make things worse.

Sitting up, Lorien looked around his prison. Instead of a dungeon, he was in a tower room with comfortable furnishings—the bed curtained against drafts and two armchairs set near the windows. A few books lay stacked on a nearby table.

Next, he tested the length of his chains from where they fastened at the head of the bed. If he was careful, he could walk around most of the room and look out the three narrow windows at the sea directly below. The bars on the windows were strong and newly installed, with no chance for the salt air to rot away at them. He rattled them anyway, for all the good it did him.

They had left him only his shirt and breeches, taking even his stockings and boots so he was barefoot on the stone floor. Not so bad in the summer, especially since someone had provided rugs underfoot, but it would be unbearably cold in the winter. If they forced him to stay that long.

Whoever had captured and imprisoned him knew his abilities well, which was a bit disconcerting.

A screen hid a chamber pot and washbasin with a pitcher of water, and he had enough time to wash the dirt from his face and arms and make use of the chamber pot before the footsteps returned, this time more of them. He flung himself onto the bed and leaned against the headboard, ostentatiously relaxed, as the door opened.

Two large guards entered first, eying him warily. They each carried a heavy warhammer, most likely made of iron as well. He smiled at them. They did not smile back.

Behind them came a woman carrying a tray piled with food, the scent of which made his mouth water. He had not eaten since the previous evening.

In her plain clothing, he at first took the woman for a maid as a guard moved the books and she set down the tray, but when she looked over at him, he knew she was no servant. Command was as bred in her bones as it was in his.

"Sit and eat," she said.

He lingered on the bed, looking her up and down with as much arrogance as he could muster. She was around his age and tall for a woman, her figure slender but rounded in the right places. Her hair was covered with an intricately tied headwrap, but a few springy black curls escaped from their confinement to tangle around her temples. She was not beautiful—comely, at best—but her bronze face and dark eyes shone with a strength of purpose that made her attractive in a stern sort of way.

"I'm not hungry," he lied. "Leave it for me to eat later."

She folded her arms and he let his eyes stray to where her breasts plumped against the pressure. Her dark eyes flared with irritation, as he had thought they would. She was clearly unused to having her orders disobeyed.

"You eat now, with the guards in the room, or you wait until morning. I do not have enough soldiers to wait upon your every whim, lordling."

He glanced out the window to see it was likely mid-afternoon. Having no desire to wait another twelve hours or more to eat again, he swung his legs from the bed with a show of reluctance and padded over to the table, chains clanking behind him. She stepped back out of reach, and he smiled at her. Her expression did not change.

"Eat," she said, and he sat down. The food was plain, but good. He observed her from beneath his eyelashes while he ate, as she watched him in turn.

"Aren't you afraid of poison?" she asked, her tone heavy with irony.

He shrugged. "It would be foolish of you to go to all this trouble to build me a personal prison, only to poison me as soon as I arrived. How long are you planning to keep me?"

"That depends on you."

"I see." He pushed the plate away and toyed with his empty cup as he leaned back, conspicuously relaxed. "Am I a hostage?"

"In part. Your father dare not attack us while we hold you."

"He might," Lorien said. "We're a bit on the outs at the moment."

The woman rolled her eyes. "Even if he wanted to attack, your brother would not allow it. Not when he knows we would present him with your head if he tried."

"I suppose so. Then what, pray tell, is my purpose here?"

She nodded to the two guards, who stepped back to flank the door.

"Your family owes mine a debt, lordling, so you are here to tutor me in magic."

His laugh was not feigned. "You can't be serious."

"I am deadly serious," she said, her tone leaving no room for him to doubt her.

"I'm afraid you have wasted your time, then. Magic cannot be taught if one does not have a talent for it."

In response, she held her hand out, palm up. A translucent sphere formed on it, whirling as it grew, golden flames flickering inside until the sphere whirled apart and the flames extinguished in mid-air with a sound like tinkling bells.

"Parlor tricks," he said dismissively, hoping his face did not show his astonishment.

"I know. But there is no one here who can teach me more." She looked at him, her dark brown eyes aflame with purpose. "*You* can teach me."

"Perhaps," he said. "Is that all?"

"You will help me build our magical defenses against your father. And then we will let you go."

His hand clenched on the cup. "You ask too much."

"You will have time to decide." She held out her hand, and he placed the cup in it. She put it back on the tray and lifted it to leave.

"Do you have my saddlebags?" he said, and she looked over her shoulder at him.

"The guards will bring them to you once I have had an opportunity to look through them and remove any dangerous items."

"Thank you," he said with heavy irony and a little bow from his seat. She left without another word, the guards following in her wake.

Lorien leaned his head back against the chair and sighed. Despite their lack of a formal introduction, he knew who she was now, or at least who her family was. It only made his current position more precarious. The Mochain clan had begun a feud with his family more than a dozen years ago, and now it appeared he was their prisoner. His father would be enraged, no doubt, but with luck his brother Tasgall's cooler temper would prevail. Lorien had no desire to lose his head thanks to one of his father's tantrums.

He took a few moments to inspect his shackles. They were well-designed, with the lock of each cuff blocked by a separate lock that attached to the chains. In order to free himself, he would need to pick eight separate locks—no, ten, because of the collar around his neck.

That left him with only one available weapon—his wits. They had never failed him yet, and he sincerely hoped this would not be the first time.

She had not expected him to be handsome.

Oh, Mirade had known he was likely not the monster he was rumored to be—after all, sorcerers were but men and women despite their powers. She ought to know, being one herself.

But she had not expected finely cut features and dark hair that tumbled to his shoulders, or piercing pale eyes that seemed to change color from gray to green to blue as he watched her. He was not a heavily muscled warrior like the men who surrounded her. Instead, his lithe build reminded her of a wildcat, coiled and prepared to pounce, and his height was intimidating enough that she had backed away before she steeled her spine. She was taller than most of the men in her keep, but he topped her by half a head more.

And his hands. Long and elegant, they were the hands of an artist or a musician… or a master sorcerer.

Mirade shook herself. It didn't matter what he looked like. It only mattered that he could teach her what she needed to know, and that he could do it before his father's army overcame her guards. She never would have taken a hostage unless she was desperate… and she was very desperate these days.

"My lady!" Mirade winced at the peremptory tone of her old nurse, but waited for the older woman to catch up as Nurse puffed her way down the hallway.

"Have you gone mad, Lady Mirade?"

"Certainly not," Mirade said coolly. "Shall we continue this in my solar?"

Grumbling, Nurse followed in her wake to the solar, Mirade deliberately slowing her steps to avoid the scolding she knew was coming. The door had barely closed behind them before Nurse whirled on her. "What have you done, Lady Mirade?"

Mirade glared down at the other woman, who did not flinch. She might be wizened and withered, her dark skin now lined with a web of wrinkles, but Nurse knew she could still demand her due deference, even from the lady of the castle.

"We were able to capture one of the Brodhans' men," Mirade said. "Their sorcerer, in fact."

Nurse snorted. "Not much of a sorcerer if you could sneak up on him."

"We were very careful," Mirade said, unsure why she felt an urge to defend the man. "He wasn't expecting an attack when he was such a short distance from his father's keep, so we took him by surprise."

"And now what is your plan, if I may ask?"

"He will instruct me in the type of magic I need to know in order to defend our keep," Mirade said coolly. "And, of course, he will be a hostage against his father attacking us before Ronek returns."

"Lord Ohrean will be on our doorstep by tomorrow eve." Nurse's voice was gloomy, but it held a thread of satisfaction at the thought of being proven right.

"Nonsense," Mirade said. "It will take at least a week for him to realize that Lord Lorien never reached the city, and another week past that to realize we must have taken him."

"And on the third week, Lord Ohrean will besiege us."

"He can besiege us, but we still hold his son. He will not dare to attack."

"The sorcerer will never cooperate. He knows you wouldn't kill him." Nurse's voice was a little doubtful, and Mirade looked away.

"I won't kill him unless his father overruns the keep, but I could make him much less comfortable than he is, and he knows it."

A guard came to the open door of the solar and stood

diffidently outside it, a pair of leather bags dangling from his hand. "I have the sorcerer's things, milady."

"Thank you." Mirade brushed past Nurse and took the bags from the man's hand.

Nurse threw up her hands. "I suppose I must allow you to do as you please, Lady Mirade. You always do." With a snort, she pivoted on her heel and turned away, firmly closing the door behind herself.

Mirade turned her attention to the saddlebags in her hand, suppressing her disquiet at Nurse's words. She had assumed his entire bag would be bespelled, but there was only the slightest resistance as she undid the ties and carefully spilled the contents onto the table, spreading them out as best she could without touching them more than necessary, wary of any magical defenses that might not be obvious. Tucked in among the shirts and breeches was a small book covered in battered brown leather.

She was luckier than she had ever dared hope. It was Lord Lorien's gramarye, the notes he used for his own personal spellwork.

Carefully, Mirade extended her hand and hovered it over the notebook's cover. To her surprise, she didn't feel any power pushing her away and, after another hesitation, she brushed her fingertips across the cover.

A shock ran up her arm, and she snatched her hand away, her fingers still tingling but... not unpleasantly? It was the strangest feeling. Not unlike the feeling when she had seen the sorcerer lounging at his ease on the bed, one long leg stretched out in front of him and the other bent to support his arm as he looked her over with those cool, calculating eyes, only to find her wanting.

Not that she wanted anything from him. Of course not.

It was merely her vanity that had made that caustic gaze sting.

Cautiously, she moved her hand back to the notebook, too curious to stop herself. It lay quiescent under her touch as she opened the cover and flipped through the pages. Perhaps it, too, was being held in check by the iron that held its master's magic at bay, but Mirade didn't think so. Any spells he had cast before his captivity ought to still be in force. Instead, she had the oddest sense of being... welcomed?

As she had assumed they would be, many of the spells were martial in nature: spells to defend a wall or break it down, spells to allow a far-seeing gaze into another's keep. The sorts of spells she would need to guard against if the Brodhans besieged them.

But here and there, scattered among the rest and growing more frequent as she turned the pages, were gentler spells. Spells to create a bubble of light around oneself or to encourage flowers to bloom before their season. Spells to seduce and charm rather than besiege and force. She found herself tracing the sketched outline of a butterfly and the drawing fluttered beneath her fingertips, ready to take flight.

With a sniff, she closed the book, though she continued to hold it. Given his reputation, she ought to have known that the Brodhan sorcerer would be prepared to use his... his wiles to get what he wanted.

Well, he would catch cold at that. There was far too much at stake for Mirade to allow herself to be swayed from her path. The future of her entire clan, perhaps their very survival, was at stake if she could not defend the keep against the Brodhans in her brother's absence. The

Lord Sorcerer Lorien would give her magic lessons, or else—

Or else...

Mirade frowned at her own weakness and tossed the book onto the nearest table. There was no use being sentimental about a man who could tear the keep down around them, stone by stone, if his magic were let loose. She must not have any compunction about destroying him before he had a chance to destroy them all.

Chapter Two

Lorien spent the first evening of his captivity scouring the room for any hint of a tool he could use to unlock his bonds, but whoever prepared the room had been thorough in removing anything that might be of use to him in escaping. If he could get close enough to the lady, he might steal a hairpin or other adornment to use as a lock-pick, but he would need to be swift and discreet. He already knew she was no fool.

He was surprised how well he slept despite his chains. There was only a tiny sliver of the sea visible from each narrow window, but he could hear it at every moment, the waves moving in and out like a giant breathing beneath the walls. He had expected the constant noise to keep him awake, but instead it had soothed him to sleep, like a lullaby in a language he didn't understand.

There was no sign of the lady the next morning, only taciturn guards more interested in watching to make sure he did not steal any utensils while he ate than in conversation. From observation, he gathered that the keep was not wealthy. Their people seemed well-fed and healthy enough, but the arms and armor of the guards were in the carefully maintained styles of a dozen years ago, at least, and their lady's dress had been faded from too many washings.

As the day dragged on without company, occasionally something would skim past his view and catch his attention. It was usually a sea bird, but sometimes a boat, sails stretched to catch the wind. He wondered what it was like to go out onto the wide ocean in one, to trust that a small craft made of wood and canvas would safely glide over the surface of the water rather than sink. But even his musings could only keep him entertained for so long.

His captor was intelligent enough to not return until the following afternoon, when he was thoroughly bored.

The door opened while he was paging through one of the books left laying on a table. It was no wonder she had been unable to progress in her magic. Lorien had left this one behind before he was eight years old.

The lady of the keep seemed no more agreeable than at their first meeting, her full mouth set into prim lines as her dark eyes pierced into him. He did not rise from his chair, knowing that the small discourtesy would nettle her. She carried a small bundle over her arm that she set onto the foot of the bed.

"Have you thought about my offer?"

"I have thought about it," he replied.

The silence stretched between them like a challenge, but he knew she would lose her patience first. She was the one in need, not him.

"And?" she finally said.

"And we should discuss it further." He tilted his head back to meet her gaze. She was the tallest woman he had ever encountered, with the top of her head reaching to the top of his ear, if he remembered correctly. If he were to kiss her plush lips, he would only need to bend his head a short distance and never risk a sore neck.

Not that he wanted to kiss her, of course.

"There is nothing to discuss," she said, frowning at him.

"I disagree. Among other things, I do not even know the name of my proposed pupil."

She glowered down at him, and he nodded to the chair across from his. After a brief hesitation, she seated herself, settling her skirts around her. She gestured to the guards, and they took up their places again at either side of the door.

"You know my name," he prodded, leaning back in his chair with assumed relaxation.

"Lorien, the Lord Sorcerer of clan Brodhan."

He made her a little bow from his seat. "I have that honor. And you are…?"

She paused for another moment and then said reluctantly, "Mirade of Mochain, sister to Lord Ronek."

As he had suspected. He bowed again. "Charmed to meet you, Lady Mirade."

She nodded in return. "And my lessons?"

He placed his elbows on the arms of the chair and steepled his fingers, the chains rattling as he moved. "I don't suppose I could talk some sense into you," he said softly, too softly for the guards to hear. "If you return me immediately, my father will only be a little angry."

She laughed, a short, sharp laugh. "And have him overrun us as soon as our hostage is safely returned to him? I thank you, no, my lord sorcerer. Now that we have you, we must keep you until… that is, we must keep you until you complete my magic lessons."

Lorien noticed the change, but said nothing. He continued gazing at her with the look that usually had people either whimpering in fear or sliding into his lap, depending on their preferences, but she did neither. She merely held his gaze, as steady as he in their battle of wills.

Even when his father discovered who had abducted him, there was no guarantee he would be able to free him. Lorien had been with his father at the Brodhans' last siege of this keep, barely sixteen and eager to help conquer their enemies, but even their combined magics had been unable to overcome the keep's natural defenses. He could still remember the expression on his father's face when the broken body of his uncle Doneach—his father's younger brother—had been returned to their side during the siege, pierced by a dozen Mochain arrows after Doneach had attempted to lead a squad to attack what seemed to be a less-defended side of the keep. The siege had only lasted another week past that.

The calculation for him was stark. He could sit in this room alone and bored for weeks on end, waiting for a rescue that might never come, with meals brought to him on a tray by people who refused to speak to him. Or he could try to gain his captor's trust and, through it, seize an opportunity to escape. It seemed the only way to do that was to teach her magic, or at least make a pretense of doing so.

"Very well," he said. "We commence tomorrow. Bring my gramarye."

"Not today?"

"No. I must decide on an approach. Tomorrow. After breakfast."

A smile as dazzling as the sun coming out from behind a cloud crossed her face and vanished again almost as quickly. "Very well. I shall call upon you for our first lesson tomorrow, then. In the meantime, I have brought you a change of clothes from your saddlebags."

"Thank you," Lorien said automatically, still spellbound by that brief smile. It transformed her, easing her stern countenance and revealing an unexpectedly whimsical gap between her front teeth. It made her almost... well, not pretty. A stronger word than that, for a strong woman.

He began to wonder exactly what he had gotten himself into.

Time to turn the tables.

As Mirade rose from her chair, the sorcerer spoke again.

"Much as I admire your thoroughness," he said, "there is something you did not take into account when you designed my fetters."

"Oh?" Mirade said. "And what was that?"

He pulled on one cuff of his shirt and slid it off his hand and down onto the chain. "There is no way for me to change my clothing. And this very pleasant prison will quickly become *un*pleasant for all of us if I must continue to wear the same clothes for weeks or months to come."

Mirade fumed silently. She hated to have him point out any flaws in her plan, but she had to admit that he was right.

"If you insist on keeping me chained hand and foot, then I can see only one option."

"Oh?"

He shrugged, and a devilish smile played on his face. "I'll have to go naked."

Mirade was able to control her expression, but not the hot flush that spread up her neck and across her face. The worst part was that the idea of having him naked and at her mercy was not nearly as repellent as it ought to be.

No, she realized a moment later, the worst part was his knowing smirk while she thought about him naked, and she scowled at him.

"My men will help you dress and undress," she said, gesturing for them to come forward even though they both frowned at her. "One will watch you while the other unlocks each chain."

"Shouldn't you stay in the room to supervise them?" He directed another of those arrogant smiles at her. "You don't know what mischief I might cause."

Mirade hesitated. He was right, damn him. She needed to remain in the room in case something went wrong.

"I will turn my back," she said. She nodded to the two guards. "Take him to where the washbasin is and let him wash. I will bring his clothes."

"Yes, milady," one of them muttered, and gave the sorcerer a shove to move him in the right direction. He moved along willingly with only a small stumble, and Mirade frowned at the chains that dragged behind him. She had not wanted to take any chances on his being able to escape, but now she wondered if she had put too much of a burden on him. Well, perhaps when she saw how he behaved after a few lessons, she could remove or reduce his chains.

Not the cuffs and collar, though. Those kept the flow of his magic in check and his strength at merely that of a man.

She selected a shirt, breeches, and smalls from what had been in his saddlebags and approached the screen. There was a low laugh from behind it—he was already trying to suborn her guards!

Without stopping to think, she stepped around the edge of the screen and halted in her tracks when she saw he had already removed his shirt and was soaping the rag left on the washstand. He looked up at the movement and smiled at her, spreading his arms.

"Have you had a good look?" he said genially. "Shall I turn around so you can examine my back as well?"

Blushing furiously, she shoved the clothes at the nearest guard. "That won't be necessary," she said coolly, and retreated to the other side of the screen, trying to stop thinking about his broad shoulders and sinewy arms and the intriguing scattering of dark hair across his naked chest. The sound of splashing water from behind the screen made the sight even harder to forget, especially when she realized he had probably stripped off his breeches as well and was standing naked with only the thin wood of the screen separating them. If she concentrated, she might be able to...

With a gasp, she turned her back to the screen, but his chuckle came through the barrier, low and intimate, as though he knew exactly what she had been tempted to do.

He had unsettled her since the moment she had seen him lounging at his ease on the bed, his shirt open at the throat and one exposed forearm propped up on his knee as he looked her over with a little smile of contempt. His tousled hair and casual attire had made him look as though they had interrupted him at bed-sport, and she could not prevent her curious mind from wondering which of the rumors that swirled around him were true.

Mirade stiffened her spine. It did not matter. Their clans were enemies. She had caused him to be seized by force and was holding him prisoner. The most she could hope for between them was that he would instruct her in magic so she could defend her people. If Lord Lorien's father attacked, she might have to execute him to protect her keep.

The very thought was enough to bring her unruly imaginings back under her control.

That evening, Mirade sat on the stool in front of her mirror and unwound her headcloth to allow the coils of her hair to spring free. She dipped her hands into the jar of scented cream on the table, rubbed a little into her hands to smooth the roughness brought by the day's work, and dampened her fingertips. One by one, she combed her fingers through her curls, straightening and separating them from each other, giving them moisture with the cream on her hands, the familiar ritual soothing her after a long day of being pulled in every possible direction by the demands of running the keep.

And a captive sorcerer who stirred up unnecessary feelings.

Bend and twist and smooth, each coil of hair bouncing back into its place. The rhythmic action helped move the cares of the day away from her mind and reminded her of her mother's patient lessons in caring for herself as well as caring for her people, even in these small ways.

With a sharp pang, Mirade remembered her parents sitting in front of the fire in the family's private rooms, talking and laughing quietly together while her father's battle-scarred hands moved gently through her mother's hair as she leaned against his knees, his touch surprisingly deft as he untangled her curls from one another, taking the cares of the day away from them both with the familiar motion. Sometimes the intimacy between them had been so intense that Mirade had had to look away.

When she had begged her mother to read her future, her response had been, *the man who walks your dreams will walk with you to the end of your lives.*

The sorcerer's face flashed into her mind again, but she ignored it as the illusion it was.

Bend and twist and smooth. Moving everything back into place before it was ruffled anew on the morrow.

Chapter Three

The next morning, Mirade found herself with the sorcerer's gramarye in her hands again, oddly reluctant to return it to him despite her promise. She told herself it was merely curiosity. The Mochain family's gramarye had been stolen by the Brodhans when they killed her father and she had not seen another since. Perhaps she ought to keep this one, in trade for the one that had been stolen.

She set the book on the edge of her mattress and paged through the spells, turning them over in her mind as she scanned them. Her fingers trailed over one in particular, an image of a flurry of butterflies emerging from a hand, and almost before she could think, one hand formed into the shape shown in the sketch while the other traced the image before her, allowing it to flutter against her fingertips for a moment before she pulled her hand away.

A multicolored cloud shot from her upturned palm in a great rush until she was surrounded by butterflies that fluttered out to every corner of the room. She hurried to open the window and shoo them out, watching as they dipped and turned on the ocean breeze in the light of the summer dawn, taking different directions until they were lost to her sight.

She looked back to where the gramarye lay sprawled on the floor, dropped in her haste to open the window. It seemed almost... reproachful. She approached it carefully and picked it up, smoothing its ruffled pages back into place until it lay closed in her hand like a cat curling up to sleep.

She shook herself at the foolish thought. It was not alive, of course, merely imbued with the sorcerer's magic and attuned to him.

A swift tap on the door of her chamber brought her attention back, and she slipped the gramarye into a pocket of her skirt as she opened the door to begin her day.

After they broke their fast in the kitchen, Nurse stood up from the opposite bench as Mirade prepared to leave, and Mirade glanced at the older woman in confusion. The rest of the women sitting around the table, including Nurse's third daughter, Firchara, suddenly found things to draw their attention to the other side of the room, gathering there to glance nervously back at the pair.

"Did you need something, Nurse?"

"I have spoken to the sorcerer, so I will come with you this morning."

"No one was supposed to speak to him except myself and the guards." Mirade knew she ought to be irritated— and she was—but her overall feeling was of resignation. Of course Nurse would not consider herself bound by the rules Mirade had set up.

"He is a well-enough looking man, I suppose," Nurse said. "Knows his manners, at least. But you ought not to be alone with him for these lessons."

"The man is chained hand and foot, Nurse. What do you expect him to do?"

"A man like that can do more than enough, even when you have him bound."

Mirade waved a dismissive hand. "He knows full well what would happen to him if I came to any harm at his hands."

"Aye, well, it's his hands I'm worried about, Lady Mirade, and what they might get up to if left alone with you."

Mirade knew she was blushing, but she still met Nurse's eyes steadily. "He's not interested."

"For a man who's not interested, he asked many questions about you." Nurse smirked at her. "And you have far too many opinions about him."

"Well, if you must come, then come now," Mirade said with ill grace. "We still have the soapmaking to supervise this afternoon, or the whole castle will reek by spring."

"Certainly, my lady," Nurse said, and Mirade turned her back on the old woman's too-knowing eyes as she led the way down the corridors to the room where the sorcerer was being held.

As they entered, the sorcerer rose from his chair and bowed low to Nurse, a courtesy that Mirade knew full well he had been withholding from her. "Good morrow, madam."

"Good morrow, my lord sorcerer." Nurse allotted him one of her rare smiles, and Mirade wondered again exactly what they had discussed, and whether she really wanted to know.

Despite his chains, he escorted Nurse to a chair in the corner that had not been there the day before, carefully positioned so that the light from the window would illuminate the older woman's needlework, and settled her into it. He glanced at Mirade as he did and she could see the smirk in his eyes as he walked back and sat down, gesturing for her to sit as well. Stubbornly, she leaned against the arm of her chair instead to keep the advantage of height over him.

"Let us begin with the basics," he said. "What is your radius?"

"My what?"

"Your radius," he said, with a touch of impatience. "The extent to which you can project your magic outward, beyond yourself."

"Oh!" Mirade said. "My grandfather called it... never mind. I think it was two leagues."

He was silent for a long moment. "That is... are you certain? That is quite a long distance."

She met his eyes with challenge. "That is what it was before my grandfather died nearly ten years ago."

"Show me."

Mirade opened her mouth to protest, to insist that there

was no need for such a demonstration with the magic she needed to learn, and then closed it again. He clearly doubted her, and she would need to prove her abilities if they were to move forward as quickly as she needed. She came to her feet, mind rapidly sifting through the possibilities until she reached the perfect one.

Closing her eyes, she took a deep breath and pictured what she wanted to fetch, making the image as clear and strong in her mind as she could. Her fingers rubbed against each other and then traced the lines of it in the air in front of her, invisibly forming the object she wanted before she opened her eyes and held her arms out, palms open.

It was heavier than she remembered it would be, cold seawater running down her forearms as she nearly dropped it. Two of the animals inside skittered across each other, their eyestalks waving in alarm at their abrupt change of scenery.

The sorcerer's startled expression as he recoiled made it all worthwhile, even though she was forced to pull the slimy thing against her front, the lobsters' claws clacking as they tried to grab at her dress through the holes in the trap.

"What *is* that thing?"

"A lobster trap," she said with assumed casualness, and turned to one of the guards. "Bring this down to Cook, will you? We can serve them for supper."

"Yes, milady," the guard said, hanging his warhammer from the loop on his belt and taking the trap from her.

Mirade turned back to the sorcerer to see him watching her with new calculation in those peculiar, changeable blue eyes.

"How far away did you reach to fetch that?"

She shrugged. "Not so very long a distance outward. It

was the distance through the water to the sea floor that was the difficult part."

"Well done," he said after a long moment, and she couldn't help her flash of pride at the words. A little smile drifted across his face, quickly suppressed, and she thought perhaps he couldn't help his reaction to her feat, either.

Nurse clucked from her chair in the corner, and Mirade and Lorien both flinched and looked away from one other.

"Lady Mirade, you have made a mess of your gown. We will need to get you changed before you can return to your other duties."

Mirade was suddenly conscious of wet wool dragging against the linen of her shift, the smell of the seawater and the faint marks of the trap where it had rested against her front. The sorcerer's eyes traveled the same path, and she thought she saw him flush a little in turn as she crossed her arms over her breasts to shield them from his prying eyes.

"Very well, Nurse," she said. "We shall see you tomorrow, my lord sorcerer."

"I look forward to it, Lady Mirade," he said, and she had the oddest feeling that he actually meant it.

It wasn't until she walked away that she realized she had not returned his gramarye.

Chapter Four

The next morning, the sorcerer cocked his head as he accepted the gramarye from Mirade's hand. "You opened it?"

Mirade felt a flush heat her cheeks. "Yes."

He continued looking at her until she felt sure that the guilty flush would set her skin on fire, then looked back at the gramarye. She had not realized how... intimate it would feel, her having read his spells, him knowing that she had read them.

He flipped through a few pages without looking at her, his chains clinking. "Did you try any of them?"

Now her skin truly *would* go aflame. "No."

Those sea-colored eyes slanted a look up at her, holding her gaze with his own. "Liar," he said softly. His long fingers stroked the cover of the book. "You should not have been able to open it at all. Not with the wards I put on it."

She shrugged, at a loss for an explanation herself. "You are held in iron. Perhaps it affects the potency of your existing spells."

"Perhaps," he echoed, but his pupils flared a bit at her choice of words, and she cursed herself. The last thing either of them needed to think about while they were together was his *potency*.

"Where is your family's gramarye, Lady Mirade, if you do not have one of your own?"

Old rage flared up, hot and fast, at the unexpected question. "Did you not know?" she said caustically. "Your father stole it."

A crackling silence fell between them for a long moment, but Mirade did not allow her challenging gaze to drop from his furious one.

"You accuse *my father* of taking your family's gramarye, Lady Mirade?" His voice was soft, deadly so. It was the worst of all insults to so much as imply that one clan would steal magical tools from another.

Mirade glared right back at him, her spine straight. "My father had the family gramarye with him when he was killed. When my grandfather located his body, it was gone."

"Anyone could have taken it. Bandits. Scavengers."

"Or your family. His murderers."

"Be very careful to whom you say such things, Lady Mirade," he growled. "I would not let many insult my family to my face."

"It's only an insult if it is not true."

"Can you prove it?"

She made a frustrated gesture in the air and glared at the puff of magic that followed it. "Of course not. Whoever killed my father made certain we would not be able to prove anything. But my grandfather knew. He tried to seek justice, but…"

Mirade whirled away. "Never mind. You will see the truth when you are ready."

She had almost been foolish enough to forget who he was.

Her enemy.

How *dare she?*

Even after the door closed behind her, Lorien continued scowling at it. The magic inside him roiled with his anger, washing against the iron that held him without an outlet. Her accusations were ridiculous, of course. Absurd. Lorien had very few illusions when it came to his father, but Lord Ohrean was not so dead to honor he would steal another clan's gramarye and make war on them when they complained.

He forced himself to return his attention to the precious gramarye in his hand, opening the cover to page through it. There did not seem to be any damage. Lady Mirade did not seem to be someone given to spite, and only a spiteful person would tamper with a sorcerer's personal gramarye. He could not help but wonder which spell she had attempted, and if it had succeeded. Using another sorcerer's spells without guidance was a chancy business, likely to backfire if one did not have the proper experience of translating them to one's own abilities. She did not appear to have suffered any ill effects, other than being as shrewish as ever.

His temper cooled as the day dragged on, and Lorien had to admit arguing with his captor had perhaps not been the wisest of ideas. If she chose not to return and to merely keep him as a hostage, it could be difficult for him to contrive a way to escape. He ought not to blame her for her harsh words. He had been barely twelve years old himself when the feud began, and she was of a similar age. She must have misunderstood or misinterpreted something the adults around her had said.

She did not return that afternoon, nor that evening, or even the next morning, and Lorien knew he would need to act to bring her back within his reach.

L ady Mirade frowned at him. "What is so important that you must have the guards summon me as though I were at your beck and call? I have duties to attend to."

"I understand you are busy," Lorien said, and attempted a winning smile. She did not return it. "I would not have bothered you otherwise. I am in need of some medical attention."

He extended his hand to her, allowing the fetter to slide down, and she took his hand in hers to examine his wrist. He had abraded his skin with the shackles for a good while to produce the welts he wanted without taking it so far as to cause a true injury.

Her eyes widened, and she pushed the fetter slightly up with her other hand, tracing the swollen area with a gentle finger.

"It does not hurt very much," he said, striving to keep his tone indifferent, "but you would not want an infection to set in if it were to be rubbed raw." He allowed his hand to remain in hers as her fingers moved over his skin, gently stroking, and he was aware of an uncomfortable surge of arousal that was not in his plan.

"I have a balm in my workroom that will help," she said.

"If you insist," he said, as she turned her attention to his other hand. It was rather pleasant to have a woman fuss over him, even more so knowing he was advancing his own plan towards escape by allowing her to do it.

It certainly had nothing to do with him liking the feel of her hands on him. Not at all.

She stepped out of the room to fetch the balm and he settled back into the chair, watching the bored guards from the corner of his eye and wondering where Nurse was. It was going to be difficult for him to seduce Lady Mirade with two sets of eyes on them at all times. He would need to convince her they required more privacy for the magic lessons once they began in earnest.

When Mirade returned, she held her hand out to the guard. "Give me the keys to his fetters."

The guard looked at Lorien, then back at Mirade. "Is that safe, milady?"

Lorien gave the man his most winsome smile, but it didn't seem to reassure him much. Mirade kept her hand out.

"You are both here. He would not be so foolish as to try to harm me while you are armed with iron. Are you?" she said, turning to Lorien.

"Certainly not," he said. "I like my head where it is."

"You see? He is a sensible man."

Lorien smiled at her despite a stab of anger. She would pay for that jibe later, oh yes. But not now, not when the guards hovered nearby.

She set the jar that contained the balm onto the table and reached for his hand. He watched as she unlocked first the chain and then the fetter beneath it. As he had thought, it required two separate keys, and once again he wished Mirade were less clever. She had planned his imprisonment well.

As the shackle fell away, he felt his power surge from his heart down to his hand, but he pulled it back. He would not be able to disarm the guards before they could strike, not while the rest of the chains still dampened his magic.

Mirade set the fetter and chain onto the table and opened the jar of balm. It had a sharp but not unpleasant scent, like herbs and new-cut hay, and she dipped two fingers into it before taking hold of his hand.

"This may sting a bit at first," she murmured, "but then it will feel cool and bring a little numbness."

"All right," he said, and watched her sensitive fingers stroke across his skin. His scalp drew tight as a fragment of his mind imagined how her hands would feel on other parts of his body, but he did his best to keep his expression blank. It only took a sidelong glance at one of the scowling guards to see that he was not as successful as he hoped. Fortunately, Mirade was oblivious as she carefully rubbed the balm in, covering every inch of his wrist before snapping the shackle and chain back on.

"Only four more to go," Mirade said, and he bit back a laugh. Her care was more torturous than the shackles, a test of endurance as she moved to his other wrist and repeated the procedure. She was far more thorough than was good for his composure, her balm-slicked fingers gliding easily around his wrist, and he resisted the urge to pull away.

Next, she leaned forward and unlocked the chain and

collar around his neck. The surge of magic was stronger now, harder to hold back, but he forced it down and instead watched the guards watching him from over her shoulder, trying to ignore how her breasts swayed dangerously close to him as she moved. Her hands stroked up and down and all around his throat before she re-locked the collar and chain.

He didn't begin to sweat until she knelt at his feet, taking one onto her lap as she fiddled with the locks.

"Ticklish?" she said as she worked.

Lorien avoided the guard's fulminating eye as he shifted in his seat and crossed his arms across his lap as casually as he could manage. "Something like that."

Her plump thighs cradled the sole of his bare foot, and he could feel the warmth of her body radiating through her gown. Her deft fingers freed his ankle and his foot twitched as she smoothed the balm over it. The contrast between her warm fingers and the cooling balm as she knelt before him was almost too much, and he desperately tried to think of unpleasant things before he burst out of his breeches.

"Almost done," she said, as she re-locked the shackle and chain and took hold of his other foot.

"Good," he growled, hoping he sounded more angry than aroused. The vision of her sliding those skilled hands up his thighs to where they could really do him some good was almost too vivid, especially when she bent her head to examine his foot more closely, revealing her soft nape where a few dark curls had escaped her headwrap. He could cup his hand around that vulnerable spot, tug her head a little closer as she unbuttoned his breeches and...

"I should have looked at this earlier," she said. "I am sorry."

He shrugged, too aware of their audience to produce a more polite response. "Apology accepted. Finish, if you please."

She jerked a little at his arrogant tone, but he needed her to stand up and move away so he could get himself back under control. He tried taking a few deep breaths to calm himself, but only drew in the scent of her, brisk and clean and herbal like the balm, but with an underlying note of woman.

With a few quick motions, she re-fastened the last shackle and chain and stood, frowning down at him. "I'll check it again in a few days, but the balm should help. Should I leave it here?"

"If you wish." He knew he was being rude, but he needed her to leave because her every motion, her every word, was only arousing him more, and there was nothing he could do about it while two guards armed with iron stood beside her, with more guards beyond the door.

She could not have designed a more exquisite torture if she had tried, and it was all the more torturous knowing that she had no idea the effect she was having on him.

He dreamed of Mirade that night.

In the dream, she again knelt between his outspread legs, the guards missing from the scene but his chains still in place. They were heavier in the dream, pinning his wrists to the arms of the chair as she slowly stroked her hands up his thighs until they hovered just above where his aching erection strained against the buttons of his breeches. She looked up at him with a wicked sparkle in her dark eyes as his hips bucked upwards.

"Say 'please,'" she said, and a smile turned up the corners of her plump lips, revealing the charming little gap between her front teeth.

"Please," he said. "Please, Mirade."

Her fingers reached out to unfasten his buttons, fighting a little until at last the pressure was released and he lay bare before her.

With a pleased murmur, she reached out to grasp his cock, and he groaned again, letting his head fall forward to watch as she stroked him. "Yes, like that. Just like that."

He watched her through half-lidded eyes as her hand moved, letting her tease and play as she liked. She slid closer and, with a flirtatious glance up at him, bent her head to take him in her mouth, her warm breath brushing against the head of his cock as her lips opened...

And he woke up, aching and fully aroused and furious with both himself and her. The shuffle of a footstep outside the door told him that there was at least one guard outside, avidly listening for anything happening inside the room. Lorien rolled onto his side to face away from the door and took himself in hand, seething with resentment at the situation but unable to stop himself from pretending that his own hand was hers as he finished the job, spilling his seed onto the sheets and burying his face in the pillow to smother his groan.

She would pay for this humiliation. Oh, yes, she would.

M irade startled awake from the dream, her heart racing as she gazed out into the dark. It was night in her own bedchamber, not broad daylight in the lord sorcerer's room as she knelt in front of her prisoner and unbuttoned him while he watched her with avid eyes and urged her on with hoarse, wanting words.

It was ridiculous of her to dream such things. Madness. He was the son of her clan's greatest enemy, the one that sought to destroy her and her people. No amount of charm and sculpted features and strong arms should change any of that.

He was her guest and tutor for a short time, nothing more. For all she knew, her brother would shortly return with a betrothal contract in hand, and she would be obliged to leave her keep behind in order to save her people. There was no point in becoming attached to a man she could have no future with.

She told herself that, and yet it did not help her burning body fall back asleep.

Chapter Five

Mirade was not quite sure how she brought herself to face the sorcerer with his breakfast the next day, though she tried to compensate by being even more brisk in her manner. It was unnerving to have his gaze settle on her so often as she moved about the room, but he did not seem threatening or hostile. He seemed... thoughtful. Puzzled. As though he was also trying to understand this unwanted attraction between them.

Because she could no longer persuade herself that the attraction was solely on her side and thus easily ignored. No wonder Nurse had tried to warn her.

"Is it truly necessary for me to wear these chains as well as the shackles?"

Mirade turned to discover him looking at her. Once he knew he had her attention, he shook his wrist, sending the chain clanking.

"Among other things, they make it difficult to sleep. I keep rolling over onto them and waking myself up."

Mirade frowned, uncertain whether it was at him or herself. She had to admit that perhaps she had overdone the chains, given his fearsome reputation. The shackles alone should keep his magic in check—the chains were more to limit his movement and make it more difficult to escape.

There was another reason to lighten his imprisonment, of course. Doing so could make him more friendly towards her, more inclined to teach her the spells she needed to know. She needed to balance that with the possibility it would make it easier for him to escape if he were less burdened.

She looked over at the captain of the guard, who appeared far less willing to take the chance than she was.

"Let me consider it," she said, and the sorcerer grunted in response.

"Tell me about the Mochain gramarye. Where was it lost?"

"It was not lost," she said, knowing that her voice was tight. "It was stolen."

He waved his hand impatiently. "Where did it happen?"

"You know as well as I do that it was while my father was traveling close to the border between our lands."

"On Brodhan land."

"On the road, which belongs to no man."

"And he was attacked by bandits."

"By your father's men."

"Repeating what you were told will not make it true," he said.

"Unless you were there when my father died, my lord sorcerer, the same applies to you."

He studied her face for a long moment before silently

conceding her point with a nod. "The gramarye disappeared. Could your grandfather not locate it?"

She closed her eyes for a moment, pushing through the memories. "No. He cast many seeking spells, but the closest he could get was to see that it was inside the borders of your father's lands."

"So it could have been anyone within those lands. Even a bandit."

Mirade repressed the urge to stamp her foot at his stubbornness. "Not just anyone. Someone who knew what it was and could bespell it to remain hidden. We combined our powers more than once, my grandfather and I, but could not get past the wards that your father set up."

"You still have no proof it was my father who stole it."

She glared down at him, wanting to grasp those broad shoulders and shake him out of his certainty. "We cast one more spell together when your father last besieged us, before the fever took my grandfather. The gramarye was *there*, with him. With your father."

"You must have been mistaken."

"Must we?" she said. "Or are you the one who is mistaken?"

Impatiently, she picked up the tray and examined it before holding her hand out.

"The spoon."

A tiny smile quirked at the corner of his firm lips. "It was worth a try."

He pulled the spoon from some recess of the chair and extended it to her, but held on for a long moment when she tried to take it.

"You cannot keep me here forever, Lady Mirade."

"I have no intention of doing so," she said, and pulled the spoon from his hand with a jerk that nearly unbalanced her. "The only thing I need from you is your knowledge of magic."

"Is it?" he said, and the velvet caress of the voice from her dream made her turn and flee for the door. It was only her imagination that made her think she could still feel his body heat, carried to her by the metal of the spoon.

"Lady Mirade!" he said, and his tone made her turn back. "I cannot be expected to teach you magic if you run away every time we argue."

"I am not... I have not..." Mirade bit the inside of her cheek and took a deep breath. "I will return tomorrow."

"Be sure that you do," he said, and turned to gaze out the window.

It was only by the force of will that she prevented herself from stomping her foot as she left the room.

The lady kept her promise the next day, but it took at least a week for Lorien to fully realize how difficult it was going to be to seduce a woman who was a conscientious chatelaine. The people of the keep demanded Lady Mirade's attention every minute of the day, from giving advice on their candlemaking to judging whether the fish destined for the midday meal were fresh enough. Nurse brought the messages more often than not, bustling back and forth with a gimlet eye on him as they paused in their lessons.

Of course, Nurse and the rest of the clan might be trying to keep them apart so he could not work his wicked wiles on Mirade. Even now, the older woman lurked in a corner of the room, working on more of her endless mending while the guards kept a suspicious eye on his every movement. He almost couldn't blame them. Ever since he had dreamed about her, the attraction between them seemed a living thing.

He shifted his gaze to where Mirade sat across from him with her head bent, her finger gliding across the sheet of parchment on which he had drawn a spell for her to attempt, her full lips pulled into a lopsided frown as she practiced. Even as he watched, a coil of hair escaped from her headwrap and fell forward onto her cheek. She brushed it aside impatiently, but his fingers itched to smooth it back into place himself.

Truly, he was starting to run mad.

"Are you ready?" he said, and his tone made her look up, startled.

"Yes, I suppose so."

"Then begin."

Her eyes drifted closed and her hands rose to allow her palms to rub together, the friction generating the necessary touch to activate her magic. Even as he watched, an illusion gathered in front of her, light bending and shaping around her power until the trunk of a tree appeared. A bit fuzzy, and prone to having bits fade in and out, but unmistakably a tree.

He stretched his hand out to touch it, and it passed through the illusion with only a little trouble. He frowned.

"Let go."

She released the illusion and opened her eyes to frown back at him.

"You must learn to open your eyes once you feel the illusion begin to form," he said. "How can you judge your illusion if you are unable to see it?"

She sniffed, but accepted his criticism with a curt nod. From her corner, Nurse sighed, and they turned to look at her.

"What is it?" Mirade asked.

"Nothing much," Nurse said. "Only my fingers grow weary of working on your dowry linens."

Nurse looked straight at Lorien, who glanced at Mirade's guilty countenance and then away.

He felt an odd twinge at the knowledge that Mirade had lied to him, had been lying to him by omission since they had met. *She was betrothed.*

Nurse's eyes were boring into him, so he turned to the older woman with what he hoped would pass as a careless smile. "I had not realized that Lady Mirade is betrothed."

"I am… I mean, I am *not*," Mirade blurted out, and he looked back at her. A flush warmed her tawny skin, and she looked away. "I… I will be. When my brother returns."

"And who is the lucky man, may I ask?"

"It's… um, well…"

That unnamed twinge of emotion grew stronger. "You don't know?"

"There are three possibilities," she said a little weakly. "Ronek needed to speak with each of them."

"I see your brother continues to play as many sides off each other as he can."

"He does what he must, as we all do. He is deciding

which will be the best alliance to protect us from the Brodhans."

"And meanwhile, you wait here for him," he said, now aware that it was anger that was rising in him. Anger on her behalf. "Taking care of everything the keep and your people need while he gallivants around the countryside trying to sell you like a side of beef."

"That's not fair!"

"Not to you, it isn't." He willed her to look at him, and after a long moment, she did, seemingly compelled by the same force that drove his anger, her eyes dark and deep enough for a man to drown in. His voice lowered to a murmur Nurse could not overhear. "You deserve better than that, Mirade."

"Lady Mirade," she said, but her own voice was barely above a whisper. "You must call me Lady Mirade."

He suppressed an ironic smile at the demand that came too late. "If you insist. Lady Mirade."

"I do insist," she said, rising to her feet and raising her voice back to its normal level. "Because you can never be more to me than my prisoner."

He looked back at her, meeting her challenging gaze with his own. Finally, he said, "I understand."

Mirade nodded and swept out of the room with Nurse at her heels, her head held high in that way he had learned was her attempt to regain her composure.

He stood and turned his back to the door as the guards followed the women out and locked it behind themselves. There was no reason for him to feel any sense of loss at her words. He had no claim on her, nor she on him. None at all.

"Why did you tell him that?" Mirade hissed to Nurse as they walked away.

"It is the truth, is it not?"

"Why does he deserve the truth? Is he not our enemy?"

Nurse stopped and tugged Mirade into a small alcove, out of sight of the passers-by. She searched Mirade's face with her eyes, and Mirade shifted uncomfortably under that all-knowing gaze. Even before her own mother's death, Nurse had been as a second mother to her and Ronek. They never would have survived the hardships brought on by the feud if not for Nurse's steadfast support and advice. When she could have retired into honored widowhood after her husband's death in the siege, she had returned to the castle and what she felt was her duty.

"I do not have the gift of prophecy that your own mother did, Lady Mirade," Nurse said. "Nor even that of your brother. But there is a grave danger between you and the Lord Sorcerer. Danger to both of you. I would be remiss in my duties to not advise you to be cautious, both with your person and your emotions."

"He would never hurt me," Mirade protested, though she wondered how she could be so sure, so soon. Nurse only shook her head.

"It might not even be something one of you does to the other with intention. It may merely… happen. Guard yourself, my lady."

Mirade nodded and then, impulsively, leaned forward to kiss Nurse on the cheek. "Thank you, Nurse. I do appreciate your care, and your advice, even when I do not follow it."

Nurse only shook her head and brushed past Mirade to continue on her way, leaving Mirade alone with her thoughts.

Chapter Six

As night fell, Lorien folded his arms beneath his head, finally ready to examine the thoughts that had plagued him since the afternoon. It had been an unpleasant jolt to hear that Mirade was to be betrothed, and he was not sure he wanted to examine why that was. He did like her, it was true. When he could get her to let a little of her guard down, he saw glimpses of the personality she showed to her own people: warm, compassionate, intelligent. Even witty, when the mood struck her.

Knowing all of that was to be given to a stranger who would see her only as a commodity, the lock to keep an alliance in place, made him angrier than he had expected. Perhaps… jealous?

That was a ridiculous thought. He frowned at the ceiling. What was there for him to be jealous of? They could never wed. Their clans were enemies, and long-standing ones at that. Their families had been actively feuding since the two of them were mere children. A marriage alliance between them could not possibly mend the breach between their two peoples.

Though if he were honest with himself, he thought less about how an alliance between their clans would bring peace and more about having Mirade in his bed at night. Every night. With no barriers between them. Mirade managing his keep and his life with the same warm efficiency that she managed her brother's keep.

Mirade as the mother of his children.

He sat up abruptly. *That* was most certainly a road he did not want to travel down. There was no purpose in mooning like a schoolboy about a future that could never happen. Lorien needed to focus his mind on escaping from Mirade, not on how to keep her by his side. One of those things was impossible, and it was not the escape.

The sea was calm tonight, waves lapping at the rocks below rather than pounding against them. Moonlight traced its way across the floor, but his restlessness stayed.

He tugged fretfully on his wrist shackle, but of course to no avail. Not being able to use his magic was far more frustrating than Lorien had realized it would be. He felt agitated, bottled up, and it was not only his imprisonment. His power was being thwarted by the shackles, and it was like having an itch that started when one was least able to scratch it.

He was reluctant to sleep, because his mind kept drifting to Mirade, another itch he could not scratch without disaster.

In waking life, anyway.

He stilled, listening to the lapping of the waves and the faint whistle of the wind outside his window.

Did he dare?

To soothe his conscience, he reminded himself that he suspected they had already shared at least one dream. The dream he had had the night she rubbed the balm on his skin had been far more vivid than an ordinary dream, and he seemed to recall she had been red-faced and aloof the next morning. Perhaps she had experienced the same dream and been embarrassed by it.

It was not that he *wished* to dream with her, he reassured himself. He wanted to see if he *could* draw her into the dream with him, if he could access enough of his magic to do so despite the iron that bound him.

It was strictly in the nature of an experiment.

Lorien lay back down, refolding his arms beneath his head and settling the wrist and neck chains against the top of the bedframe. He closed his eyes, consciously relaxing his body, lulling himself to sleep. And to dream.

As one dream melted into another, Mirade found herself laying in a summer meadow, grasses and wildflowers swaying in the warm breeze that shimmered over her. In the way of dreams, she was naked but unconcerned about it. She stretched luxuriantly, feeling the soft wool of a blanket beneath the skin of her back.

"You're awake," a deep voice said next to her.

She rolled to her side and was unsurprised to find Lorien lying next to her, equally naked in the summer sun, arms folded behind his head as he gazed up at the sky. She took a long moment to admire him as he lay there, sleek and lean as a wildcat, and with as much coiled power as the animal possessed.

"Yes," she said, and he rolled onto his side to face her. She reached out to smooth his unruly hair back from his forehead, and he smiled at her, his pale eyes glowing with admiration.

"You're beautiful," he said, and leaned down to kiss her, gathering her close so they pressed together from chest to hip, her arms looped around him. The skin of his back and shoulders was like satin under her hand, smoothness over taut muscles, and his half-erect cock began to grow and swell between their bodies.

His hand slid down her back to her bottom, and she raised her leg to drape across his hip in invitation. He purred his approval, hand sliding down the inside of her thigh to her knee before stroking its way back up, teasing fingers staying just out of reach until she pushed down impatiently and then sighed as he parted her damp folds and began to caress her in a rhythm that stole her breath.

"Do you like that?" he murmured, and she kissed him again for her answer, her hips surging against him as he played with her. It all spun together into a tapestry of sensual pleasures: the scent of the wildflowers, the sun on her skin, mouths and tongues tangling, Lorien's knowing hands matching her increasing urgency until every sensation coiled together to form a glorious burst of pleasure...

And she woke up, the orgasm echoing through her body even as she realized she was alone in her own bed.

Mirade sat up in alarm and looked around, but he was not in the room with her. No one was. It had all been a dream. Nothing more.

Or was it? It had been far more vivid than an ordinary

dream. She could swear she felt his hands on her even now, as though he had only just lifted them away from her sensitized flesh.

It was impossible. The iron that bound him would bind his magic as well.

Wouldn't it?

She fell back asleep still wrestling with the dilemma.

"**Y**ou must stop at once."

Lorien smothered the sly smile that tried to cross his face and instead arranged his expression into the most innocent one he could manage before he raised his head to look at Mirade. "I beg your pardon?"

She was all but vibrating with indignation as she stood before him. Every line of her gown and headwrap was in place, but he now knew from their shared dream what beauty they hid from him and the rest of the world.

"How are you able to control my dreams?"

"I cannot," he admitted. "That is what you must understand about magic, Lady Mirade. You cannot force it to work. You must use persuasion. You could have taken control of the dream at any time if you had chosen to do so, but you did not."

Her mouth opened and then closed again, and he knew he had scored a point. If she had been disgusted or outraged by their shared dream, she could easily have ended or changed it.

But she had not, and remembering how demanding yet yielding she had been was making him wonder again what they would be like together in waking time, with no restraints between them.

They would probably burn down any house that tried to contain them.

"I have you chained in iron. How can you still use magic?"

Lorien shook his wrists at her, making the chains clatter. "Iron does not *remove* magic, Lady Mirade. It only dams it up. If you stop up the mouth of a brook, does the water behind the dam evaporate, or does it collect?"

"So your power is still there."

"It is there, but I cannot access it. Not consciously. Dream time is different. Even people with no talent for magic can have experiences of magic in dreams."

She shook her head. "It does not matter. You must not do it again."

"I will do my best," he said. "But it is difficult to control one's dream-wanderings. You will need to do your part and stay out of my dreams as well."

She glared at him, and he grinned back.

"Let us speak of other things," he said. "When does your brother return?"

"That is no business of yours, sorcerer."

"It seems to be very much my business, since that is when I would be returned to my father, is it not?"

Her eyes fell from his and she moved to the window. "Of course."

To his own surprise, he said, "Let us say for a moment that my father does have your gramarye."

She whirled on him, stubborn chin held high. "He does."

He raised a hand. "I am conceding the point. What then? What do you plan to do with it if you recover it?"

Her stern face softened for a moment as she gazed out the window at the sea below. "If I recover it, I can not only protect the keep, we would be able to return to our voyages."

"Voyages?"

"When my father was young—before the feud started, when my grandfather was still alive—he would lead our people on trading voyages to the southern seas, where the air is warm nearly all the time." She gestured to one of the carpets on the floor. "He brought back that rug, and my mother as his wife. She was the daughter of a merchant with whom he was negotiating, and my father decided to negotiate her bride-price as well. My grandfather was not best pleased that my father used his money to obtain a wife rather than goods that could be traded or sold, but he was soon reconciled to their marriage."

"And what did your mother think?"

"She was happy," she said, her voice a little dreamy with remembrance. "They were happy together, though she would complain about the cold every winter and pretend to threaten to return to her father unless we built the fires up."

Mirade looked back at him, swallowing hard before turning back to the window. "When my father was killed, she took it hard. I don't think that she would have succumbed to the fever if she had not already been weakened by that loss."

Lorien's hand reached of its own accord to comfort her, but he forced it back down when the rattle of his chains alerted him. "I'm sorry," he said after a moment.

"If I had the gramarye, I would be able to protect both the keep and the ships, and the Mochains would be prosperous again, not scratching out an existence from the land and the bay as we are now. We were never meant to be bound to the shore."

"You truly think that my father still has your gramarye?"

"I know that he does."

"How do you know that whoever stole it did not destroy it?"

He could almost hear her roll her eyes at the foolish question. "I can still feel its power, of course. I would know if it had been destroyed."

"And what happens to me if my father arrives without your gramarye in hand?"

She turned to look at him, her dark eyes unfathomable. "I don't know."

After leaving Lorien's room, Mirade's reluctant steps took her to the top of the battlements that faced out towards the countryside. The captain of the guard nodded to her as she took her place beside him to survey the scene.

Iron shackles should have prevented the sorcerer from being able to make any prophecies, and yet the forces led by Lorien's father had in fact arrived, entrenched at their very doorstep, prevented from coming closer only by the difficulty of the paths and the skills of her archers. She heaved a deep sigh. The Brodhan forces could not cross the narrow causeway to the keep without being massacred, but neither could her people leave. There was another, secret passage, but only a few could use it at a time.

"How long have they been there?"

"About half a day." The captain squinted into the sun.

"We are watching them, of course, but they seem to have settled in for a siege rather than planning an invasion."

"Of course they have," Mirade said. Both sides knew only a fool would try to seize the keep outright. The narrow paths and looming cliffs meant an invading force would have to approach with its men trapped in a bottleneck, easily picked off by her archers if they were not hacked to death by her swordsmen.

But they could be besieged, and had been before. Mirade still had the occasional nightmare about the last one. The stillness of the castle. Her mother's final illness. The heavy dread that drenched every corner as they waited to see if the Brodhans could formulate a strategy to overcome the keep's natural defenses in the absence of magical ones.

Her vow to prevent such a thing from ever happening to her people again seemed only to have led them back to the same result.

When she cast her consciousness outward, she could feel the faint signature of the Mochain gramarye in the opposition lines. Someone on the other side had brought it, just as they had brought it to the previous confrontation a dozen years ago.

"We are supplied to withstand a siege," she said aloud. "Aren't we?"

"Yes, milady. For a few weeks."

"Very well." She pushed back from where she leaned against the parapet with a bravado she did not feel. "The sorcerer will have served his purpose by then, and we can return him to his father, no harm done."

"If you say so, milady." The captain's tone was not quite mutinous, but Mirade gave him a hard look before she turned to head back down the stairs to tend to her other duties.

With luck, Ronek would return with a troop of allies at his back before they ran out of supplies. If they were unlucky…

She refused to think what would happen if they were unlucky.

Chapter Seven

The days soon settled into a routine. Mirade would come to him with his breakfast, tidy the room as he ate, and then their lessons would begin. He had not realized how satisfying it would be to help someone else learn magic, to see Mirade grow in confidence and push her skills further with each session.

By her conversation, it seemed the gift of her material magic came from her father's side, but the power that underlay it came from her mother. Once her father was gone, her grandfather had not possessed the knowledge to help her grow, and her mother's talent had lay in prophecy, not material magic. It was no surprise her magic had stagnated, but now her abilities grew by leaps and bounds with a proper teacher.

He began to recognize the individual guards, though they remained as wary and sullen as ever, and would try to draw them out without success. They were protective of their lady, and he could not blame them, given what his plans were.

Lorien was careful not to dream-walk again, though the temptation was high, and it soon paid off when a frowning captain of the guard removed the chains from his wrists and ankles at Mirade's direction, leaving only the chain that fastened his collar to the wall.

"I would not wish you to suffer from restless nights again, my lord sorcerer," Mirade said, and he had to bite the inside of his cheek to suppress his grin at her daring to openly taunt him with his actions in dreamtime.

The tiny step towards freedom only made him more restless to escape and, paradoxically, more reluctant to do so. His father would grow angrier with each passing day he was a captive, and ask more and more troublesome questions about why Lorien had been unable to free himself, especially when he found himself within arm's reach of his captor for several hours each day.

It was time to try sterner measures to gain his release, and she trusted him just enough that he should be able to get close enough to try them.

"You ou will not be able to cast a spell to shield the keep and your lands all at once," he told her the next day, after Nurse had left the room on another errand. "You must start small. Such as with this room."

She looked at him for a long moment before, reluctantly, she turned to the guards. "Wait outside."

"But, milady…"

"I will be safe enough," Mirade said. "I have my magic and he does not. Wait outside."

Steps dragging, the guards left the room. One of them snapped open the small window in the door and a pair of eyes glared suspiciously at Lorien.

"Whenever you wish to begin, Lady Mirade," Lorien said, hoping his tone was indifferent enough to lull her into complacency.

She nodded and her eyes half-closed as she took a deep breath. Her hands rubbed against each other and then pushed a semi-transparent sphere outward that encompassed the room in a pale blue glow, her power shimmering and pulsing like a living thing. The shield blocked the doors and windows, leaving them in a bubble of privacy. She dropped her hands and looked at him expectantly.

Before he could reconsider, three long strides took him to stand in front of her. He wrapped both his hands around her throat, his thumbs overlapping at her windpipe. "Call your men. Tell them to unlock me."

She met his eyes, calm and defiant, keeping the shield in place. "No."

He tightened his hands just a fraction. "I could kill you right now."

Her pulse raced beneath his touch, but her face remained impassive. "You could," she said. "But if you did, my people would pull your guts out in front of your eyes before they beheaded you and sent your carcass back to your father."

His hands loosened to concede her point, but he did not remove them. With a sudden jolt, he realized how close he was standing to her, her breasts brushing against his forearms with her every inhale, the downy skin of her throat like velvet under his hands as he absently caressed her. She smelled of clean salt air and starched sheets, but with a hint of her natural musk beneath. She glared up at him with that same defiance, but a growing uncertainty clouded her eyes.

One of his arms slid down around her waist to tug her a few inches closer. His other hand moved to cup her jaw, his long fingers reaching to support the back of her head as he tilted it back.

"What do you think you're doing?" she said, but her voice came out as almost a whisper and the quiver of her body against his gave her away.

He put his lips to the hollow of her throat and dragged them along her collarbone before working his way up her neck to her delicate ear. Her natural scent was stronger here, intoxicating him as it mixed with the soap she had used to wash that morning, and he nipped at her earlobe. Her head sagged to the side, giving him better access as she swayed towards him, and he smothered his smile against her skin as he kissed the hollow between her jaw and her ear.

She raised her hands to press against his chest, but they lingered, stroking his skin through the thin fabric of his shirt.

He raised his head to look at her while he tightened the arm around her waist to pull her even closer, controlling her slight movement away with his hand on her head as he angled his mouth toward hers.

"We shouldn't do this," she whispered.

"I know," he whispered back, and settled his mouth over hers. She jolted as he changed the tilt of her head and then whimpered when he found the perfect angle that let their mouths slide together as though they had been made for each other, two halves that had been separated until this moment. Her body arched against his as her arms slid around his back to pull him closer, and he went a little mad, crushing her against him with the arm around her waist as their lips and tongues clashed and dueled and danced together.

When he found his sly hand hauling up handfuls of her skirt, he dropped the fabric as though it burned him and pushed her away. She staggered back a few steps, bracing herself against the table as she came up against it, and he had a sudden vision of sitting her on the edge, pulling up her skirts, and fucking her until she screamed her pleasure for him.

"Unless you're ready to spread your legs for me right now," he said in the steadiest voice he could manage, "you need to leave."

Her breathing steadied, and she glared at him at him. "You don't really want me."

The chains at his throat rattled as he gestured to the bulge in his breeches. "Do you want me to show you how wrong you are?"

A flush warmed her dark skin and her eyes fixed on where his erection strained against its confinement. He took another step towards her, his hands moving to his waistband, flicking the top button open as she watched, mesmerized.

"Raise your skirts or get out." She gaped at him for a moment longer, and he bellowed, "Get out!"

It was only when the shield dropped that he realized she had maintained it throughout their encounter. Stumbling, she ran to the door, turned the key in the lock, and shot through as though she were chased by demons... but she still had the presence of mind to take the key with her. He heard it grind in the lock as he sank onto the edge of the bed, rubbing his face with his hands as the guard glared in through the tiny window before closing it with a snap.

In his long history of bad ideas, that had been one of his worst. Especially since his unruly body was urging him to do that again, and finish the job, as soon as she was back within arm's reach.

Bad idea. Terrible idea.

But he was having a hard time remembering why.

Mirade ignored the questions of the guards as she half-ran through the door, turned the key, and strode away, desperate to find a private place where she could think for just a moment. She could still feel his hands on her like brands, his mouth and tongue taunting and playing with hers, his erection pressing against her belly through the layers of their clothes. The place between her legs was aching to finish what they had started, and she cursed her stupid, careless body for wanting things it could never have.

She knew she ought not to continue with their magic lessons. He naturally resented being held prisoner, and he would to try to intimidate her to convince her to set him free. But this was *her* keep, *her* home. He could not frighten her out of doing what duty required of her.

Her steps led her up the battlements to where she could look out over her lands, the siege line just out of sight though she knew it was there. On the landward side, small farms grew the crops and raised the animals that kept them all alive. To the seaward side, fishing boats went out each day, bringing in the bounty of the ocean, but she missed the days when the larger ships would return from their voyages to the southern seas, bringing the goods they could not make themselves. Their world was duller and less colorful now that none of their sailors could be spared for a voyage that would take months. Now they all needed to stay close to the harbor in case of attack.

Sometimes she felt as though her world had been constricting since the day her father had been killed. Once their ships had sailed far and wide, bringing goods and prosperity with them. Now her people barely survived on what they could grow and what they could catch in the ocean. Their world had shrunk to the village, the bay, and the keep when they had been accustomed to a much larger one.

Her uncles had visited after her father's death, her mother's brothers, insisting that her mother return with them to her homeland where they would be safe, but her mother had refused.

"This place is my children's birthright," her mother had said as Mirade and Ronek sat on either side of her. "This is the land where they were born. Why should they abandon it because of a few evil men?"

She sometimes wondered if her mother would have made a different choice if she had known she would die of the siege fever only a few years later. Prophecy had been one of her mother's gifts, one she had passed along to Ronek, so perhaps she *had* known and made her choice despite that. Perhaps Mama had realized she could not escape her fate.

Mirade took a deep breath and pushed away from the wall. Her steps were set on this path and had been since the moment she had conceived her plan to hold Lord Lorien prisoner. She must either recover the Mochain gramarye or marry away from the keep to protect it, never to return except as a visitor. And if she failed at both, she would likely be executed by Lord Ohrean for what she had done.

It was too late. She must walk this path to its end, regardless of what her fate might be.

L orien found himself left severely alone the next day, but that only gave him more time to relive the kiss. The feel of her long body against his. The intoxicating taste of her mouth. The way she had responded, arching against him as though she couldn't get close enough, needed to be even closer.

And then he had dreamed of her all night but, to his frustration, could not locate her true consciousness. He had pursued mere phantoms that slipped through his fingers as soon as he touched them. She had locked her dreams away from him, and he did not like it in the least.

When she entered his room at last the following morning, he tamped down his reaction and stayed in his seat, only raising an eyebrow as the guards followed her into the room while she carried the tray. He made a small bow to her from his seat, but she refused to meet his eyes.

"My lady Mirade."

"My lord sorcerer."

She removed the cover from the tray and he examined his breakfast. The eggs were overcooked and the porridge cold. He used the edge of the spoon to scrape some of the burned bits off the toasted bread. Clearly, word of his actions had spread to the kitchens, and Cook was making sure he knew that she, too, disapproved.

"I did not think you would be one to kiss and tell, Lady Mirade," he murmured for her ears only.

As he had hoped, her shoulders straightened and her dark eyes snapped at him as her delicately arched eyebrows drew into a thunderous frown. "I did not... 'kiss and tell,' my lord sorcerer," she hissed at him. "If my people made an assumption about what you did when we were alone together, I cannot help that."

"Did I frighten you so badly?" It was an arrogant question, he knew, but he preferred her defiance and spirit to deference and cool courtesy.

She tossed her head. "Kindly do not flatter yourself."

Lorien turned away to hide his grin. There was the Mirade he looked forward to seeing each day. He should have known a mere kiss would not cow her, even one as spectacular as the one they had shared.

"Let me know when you are ready to resume our lessons, then," he said, hiding his smile in a bite of porridge and ignoring her glare.

Chapter Eight

It was a surprise to Mirade that they could resume their lessons with only the slightest hitch. Nurse rarely left on her errands anymore, and the guards insisted on staying inside the room, but otherwise everything was the same.

Everything except the way Lorien's eyes followed her, and the way she watched him when she was almost sure he wasn't looking.

One morning, they found him standing next to one of the windows rather than in his customary chair, and he turned from it with a frown as Mirade entered the room.

"You cannot keep me in this same small room every single day."

She frowned at Lorien's querulous tone, but was secretly pleased he made no effort to hide his irritation or cozen her as he usually would. His anger was an honest emotion, and she could understand that.

"I can hardly give you the run of the keep," she replied. "Eat your breakfast."

He sat down but continued to glare at her in a way that

she assumed was supposed to intimidate her, but only made him look like a sulky boy. More than anything, it made her want to smooth his hair back from his forehead and kiss him.

Firmly, she repressed the urge. "I will think on it, my lord sorcerer."

And, just like that, the image popped into her mind. He gazed at her intently, almost as though he were trying to see what she did.

"What is it?" he asked.

"I know a place," she said slowly. "And climbing the stairs to get there will be a deal of exercise for you. But… no." She shook her head. "The walk there would expose too much of the keep."

"So blindfold me," he said, his voice reasonable despite the startling suggestion. "Or cast an enchantment."

"I could do that?"

"You must be careful. I would very much prefer that you did not blind me permanently. But, yes, there are ways."

"Like what?"

Lorien waved the piece of bread in his hand towards the charcoal and parchment on the table next to the middle window, ready for her notes. "Go and formulate one while I eat."

She was nervous about casting a spell that could have a permanent effect on him even after he reviewed and approved it, but he sat before her with surprising confidence as she lay her hands on his forehead, her fingertips rustling along the fine hairs at the edge of his temples. Remembering his previous admonishments, she deliberately kept her eyes open as she cast the spell, even though it meant gazing into his as she did. She could see the moment when his sight faded, and he flinched a little when she lay a hand on his cheek, his skin warm beneath her fingers.

"Did it work?"

"Yes," he said shortly, and she let the guards help him to his feet and re-fasten the chains to his wrists and ankles for their excursion.

She led their little procession through the corridors, seeing castle residents peek from behind doors and inside alcoves before scurrying away to report back to their friends about the mysterious captive sorcerer. As they reached the bottom of the stairs that led to the parapets, Mirade slowed her steps, forcing the guards holding Lorien's chains to slow as well.

"What is it?" Lorien said, his head turning to the side as if to hear better.

"The stairs," Mirade said. "But they are narrow."

After a moment's consideration, Mirade held her hand out for the chains. "I will lead him. Two of you walk in front, two follow behind."

Reluctantly, the captain handed the chains to her and she wound them around one hand. She took two steps forward, muttered to herself, and took Lorien's hand. She almost didn't notice how naturally their hands clasped together, their palms fitting and fingers twining into a single unit.

"Come," she said, and he followed willingly as she led him up the stairs, staying close behind as she moved from step to step until they emerged into the open air of the parapet.

"Five steps forward," she said, and led him to stand before the waist-high wall. He took in a deep breath and let it out again.

"I can smell the sea."

"We are standing above it. Almost directly above your room."

"Let me see."

After a moment's hesitation, Mirade looked in each direction. On the north end of the bay, she could see the small fishing village, but the larger harbor to the south was mostly concealed by the ridges that helped protect the keep. One would need to be able to interpret the signs to know that it stood just beyond the bend of the coast.

"All right," she said, and gestured to remove the no-see spell. Lorien blinked and then stood still for a long moment.

"I can only see a small slice of this from my windows," he said. "It's more magnificent than I realized."

They stood quiet for a long moment, and he slid his hand from hers so he could lean his elbows against the parapet.

She had not even realized they were still holding hands.

"Sailing must feel like flying," he said.

"It can," she said, "when the wind is with you. But you must try a shorter voyage before you decide to head off to the southern seas. The waves can make some people so ill that they cannot stand."

"Not you?"

"Not me. But my brother—"

He glanced over at her as she cut her words off abruptly. "I know who your brother is, Mirade. I know who *you* are."

"Still," she said, turning her gaze to look out over the ocean, "I should not tell you of his weaknesses."

"I doubt that I would be loading your brother onto a sailing ship so I could make him ill."

She shrugged, still not looking at him. "It's better if we do not know too much about each other."

"Do you know how to sail one of those?" he said, gesturing to the smallest boats skimming across the water.

"A little," she said. "I have not had much time to do it since… since the siege."

His expression darkened. "Of course. It was a foolish question."

"Our prosperity depended on the sea and our trading voyages," she said. "The feud has changed our lives far more than it has yours."

"Yet you still fight on."

"Yes. We fight on. For our land and our harbor and our keep."

"You take foolish chances."

"I have no other choice."

His eyes were steady on hers. "You still have a chance to release me. I would tell my father that you treated me well."

Mirade snorted. "You must be the only one who does not know your father's reputation." She looked away to where the fishing boats bobbed around the bay, almost able to hear the calls of the fishermen as they hauled in their nets. "No, my lord sorcerer. I will do what I must to protect my people. If that means keeping you as a hostage against your father, then so be it."

He looked at her, his face somber. "So be it," he said.

Without further speech, she re-cast the no-see spell and led the guards as they returned him to his room. There was danger in their closeness, but she couldn't seem to bring herself to put the distance between them that they needed.

As night fell, the guards unlocked the chains from Lorien's wrists and ankles and nodded their usual wary goodnight. He waited until the door closed behind them and the echo of their footsteps down the hallway faded away before he turned his back to the door to glimpse what he had tucked into the waistband of his breeches during the afternoon's excursion.

It was one of the pins that held Mirade's cuff fastened to her sleeve, a piece of metal twisted into a U-shape with a sharp point at each end.

He had lingered in captivity long enough. It was time for him to return to his own side, before he became even more entwined with Mirade and her people.

The moon was blessedly bright that night, and he was able to keep his back to the door as he maneuvered the pin, pausing every time he heard the nighttime guard's footsteps approaching and then retreating on his rounds.

At last, the fetter dropped away from his wrist, jangling as it fell to the mattress, and Lorien looked at it for a long moment. A tingle ran from his heart to his arm to his fingertips, his magic strengthening as the effects of the iron wore off.

It would not take long for him to work the locks on the other fetters, and then the one around his neck with its accompanying chain. An hour's work at most was all that stood between him and freedom.

And yet he hesitated. He knew his father. The humiliation of having his younger son held hostage for so long by their weakest enemy would be an insult to his pride almost beyond bearing. The vengeance would be legendary, with the keep and the surrounding countryside laid to waste to demonstrate such a captivity should never be attempted again. Mirade's magic was powerful, but Lorien knew his training would allow him to overcome her without much effort.

His father would execute Mirade in front of the remnants of her people—tear her guts out while she still lived and place her head on a pike to warn other clans to not test their luck. He would expect Lorien to watch, expect him to be pleased at the revenge enacted in his name.

Lorien would not be able to bear it. Not anymore.

He must find another way.

Slowly, reluctantly, he returned the fetter to his wrist and snapped it closed again. The tingle of magic faded back to the low simmer he had become almost accustomed to.

He could not be responsible for so many deaths. He could not be responsible for *her* death.

He could not escape until he knew he could prevent his father from taking revenge.

Chapter Nine

Another week passed. Mirade's ability to cast a barrier grew by the day as Lorien talked her through the process, expanding the radius of her power further and further out until she could push it past several stone walls to hover just outside the keep.

Neither spoke of the siege, but Mirade knew Lorien understood her urgency. She did not tell him of her sense that the gramarye was close by, not when they had at last reached a fragile accord.

She needed to test the barrier at the siege lines, but a strange reluctance held her back. When she could cast it, their time together would be over. She would have no more excuse to hold him.

But one morning she woke knowing it was time to put the safety of her people ahead of her own desires. Again.

Mirade led their little procession to the parapets that faced the siege lines, Lorien surrounded by guards as she removed the no-see spell from him. She took the parchment from her pocket and spread it out on the stone parapet before her. Her fingers traced the lines she had drawn, marking the village and the port and the keep, and then the line she had marked where the barrier should go.

She traced it once, and then again. She looked back over her shoulder at Lorien and he nodded reassurance.

Mirade took a deep breath and let the magic flow out the way he had taught her, relaxing into it and then directing it to where she pictured the barrier. The energy rose out of the ground in a shimmer like summer heat on the sand, rising above the heads of the men who stood inside it, out of reach of the Brodhan archers.

At the signal, the guardsmen pushed at it, to no avail. They struck at it with their swords, but to no purpose. Even an iron warhammer did nothing more than cause the barrier to bend around it and recoil back.

The barrier held.

Jaw dropped, Mirade turned to Lorien, who grinned at her. "It worked."

"It did," he said, his face alight with pride, and before she could stop to think, she crossed the distance between them and flung herself into his outstretched arms.

He caught her by the waist and lifted her to whirl her around as she wrapped her arms around his neck, his chains shifting and sliding against her skirts. "It worked!"

"I knew you could do it," he said. "You only lacked the confidence."

She laughed down at him, and then was abruptly aware of the spectacle they were making of themselves. "Put me down," she said, knowing her voice was a little breathless.

His grin turned sly as he lowered her slowly, their bodies only a hair's-breadth apart until she was back on her feet with his hands still on her hips as though they belonged there. She took a deep breath and stepped back, breaking his hold. He let her go, his hands dropping away until they rested back by his sides, the iron of his fetters gleaming dully in the sunlight.

She looked around to discover her men were carefully looking everywhere but at the two of them, and she flushed guiltily. In the joy of the moment, she had forgotten they were not alone. She had forgotten her goal was to protect the keep. She had thought only of what Lorien's reaction would be to her feat, how proud he would be of her, and he had not disappointed her.

She looked back down at the barrier, the faint shimmer visible even from her position on the parapets, and knew her time with Lorien was nearly over, whether she wanted it to be or not.

They were both silent as the guards returned Lorien to his room. She stepped inside just behind him and closed the door before the guards could enter, her back to it as the guards muttered outside. Without stopping to consider, she allowed a shield to slide out from herself, enclosing them in a bubble of privacy as Lorien watched, neither of them moving more than a step or two from the door as she drifted closer to him.

"I will need to return you to your father soon," she said.

"Agreed," Lorien said.

Mirade took another step towards him. He stood his ground, his face impassive, his changeable eyes wary and vulnerable. She said, "I do have a difficulty, though."

"And what is that?" She could see the way his throat moved as she took another step closer, and had a sudden urge to run her mouth along his neck to see if he liked it as much as she had.

"I don't want to let you go."

She raised her hands to slip them around his neck, but he caught her wrists with a quick motion that startled her, chains rattling as he moved.

"Don't start anything you're unwilling to finish, Lady Mirade," he said. There was a rasp of arousal in his deep voice, and she smiled at him.

"Kiss me."

His eyes searched hers for a long moment until, with a groan, he pulled her against him. Her arms twined around his neck with a will of their own and she opened her mouth to his for a long moment before she pulled away to run her mouth and tongue along his throat, the iron collar chilly against her cheek. He jerked against her, and his head fell back against the wall with a thump, giving her more access.

"Did you like that?" she whispered, and dragged her mouth back down towards his collarbone.

"Again."

His hands tightened on her hips and he let out a small, wild sound as she kissed her way back up the other side of his neck, nipping at the vulnerable skin just under his jaw. He smelled delicious, like wood smoke and sea salt, and she inhaled his scent greedily as she worked her mouth back down to the junction between shoulder and neck, testing it with the edges of her teeth.

Slowly, his hands glided up her waist and ribcage to hover just beneath her aching breasts, and she arched her back to encourage him to continue higher. Instead, he dipped his head for another kiss, still keeping his hands a teasing distance away from where she needed them.

Without conscious thought, she used her magic to nudge his hands up to cup her breasts, and he chuckled against her mouth before pulling back a fraction of an inch.

"Greedy, are we?" he murmured, and the rumble of his voice sent a shiver down her spine that was only surpassed by the moan that tried to escape her lips as he moved his thumbs to rub across her nipples, stroking them into taut buds that begged for another touch. Her hands tangled in his hair, keeping their mouths fused to smother the sound of her pleasure as he continued caressing her with slow, deliberate strokes that began to melt her knees.

A sharp rap at the door made her jerk away in surprise and retreat several steps away. His hands clutched out towards her for a moment before he clenched them and dropped them back down to his sides. She took a long moment to gaze at him, his pale skin flushed with arousal, his sea-blue eyes so dilated they were almost black as he looked at her with a gaze like a wolf's.

"Lady Mirade?" a guard said.

She cleared her throat and said, in the steadiest voice she could manage, "Yes?"

"Cook needs to speak to you."

"Now?"

"Yes, my lady."

Even as she watched, Lorien calmed, his breathing evening out. He smoothed his tangled hair back from his face and turned a sharp-edged smile on her.

"You may want me to stay," he said, "But how would your people feel about the matter?"

Mirade dropped the shield and fled before she had to

answer his question. She evaded the knowing eyes of the guards as she passed, half-running down the stairs to the kitchen, even though she knew Cook would have no question for her.

The guards were protecting her from herself. She reminded herself of that again. And again.

If she repeated it enough times, perhaps she might believe it.

Lorien's knees were still a little shaky as he lowered himself into Nurse's usual chair by the window and stared unseeingly out at the ocean below.

His father would consider teaching Mirade to withstand his siege to be treason, but Lorien could not bring himself to regret it. Between Mirade's joy in her own powers and his pride in her skill, he could no longer think in terms of whether something was good for the Brodhans or good for the Mochains, or why something that was good for the one must always be bad for the other.

Now he knew how his family's actions had changed Mirade's life, and the life of her family and clan. Of the desperation that sent a brother on a mission to use his sister's hand in marriage to sweeten an alliance that would save their people, and the desperation that had prompted Mirade to abduct him to teach her magic.

Unless the Mochain gramarye could be found, Lorien did not see any way free from the trap he and Mirade found themselves in, stuck on opposite sides of a feud with no way across the chasm between them.

Chapter Ten

Mirade ought not to have been surprised when the parley request arrived, but she was.

The message came under a white flag of truce, carried to her by the captain of her guard, who watched as she read it.

"Will you go, my lady?"

She read it again. The words were spare, but she still examined them for every nuance, every clue hidden in them.

"I think I must. To turn down an offer to settle things peacefully would only make our situation worse."

The man braced himself. "We will stand behind you, my lady."

"Thank you." Mirade turned to walk back to her chambers, her mind whirling.

If only Ronek was here. He had always been more diplomatic than she was, more willing to compromise, but unless he appeared before morning, she would need to do the negotiations herself.

If all went well on the morrow, Lorien could be back with his own side by evening.

If all went well, she would never see him again.

Late that night, Lorien gave up on sleep and instead tried to read a book by the single candle that was still lit. He looked up as the door opened and Mirade slipped inside like a wraith. She was still dressed for daytime, but with her hair uncovered, springing from her head in exuberant coils like it had in their mutual dream, like she had released something within herself. There was a click as she re-locked the door.

"What is it?" he asked.

She took a deep breath. "Your brother is here. He's asked us to parley."

His eyebrows rose. "Tasgall is here? Within the castle?"

"Outside the gates. We're to talk tomorrow."

"I see." He set his book aside. "So I could be free as soon as tomorrow."

"Depending on what your brother says, yes." She took another step closer to him. "You could be back with your own family as soon as tomorrow evening."

He was not ready, yet time and circumstance had rushed in upon them. It was only now, at this moment, he realized he loved her.

He held one hand out to her. "Come here."

After a slight hesitation, she obeyed, taking his hand. He used the leverage to pull her down to sit in his lap, her head resting naturally within the curve of his shoulder as she leaned against him, forehead against his throat. One of her hands came up to toy with the collar of his shirt as his arms went around her to hold her close.

He brushed his lips against her temple, breathing in her scent and letting her curls tickle his nose. "We knew this day was coming. You could not have held me here forever."

She pressed herself against him, one hand sliding up to his neck and her other arm curving around his shoulder. "I know."

They stayed like that for a long time, hearts beating together, until she sighed and he braced himself to let her go.

Instead, she pulled his head down to hers and kissed him with a frantic urgency that quickly flared into passion. In his arms, she was all soft yielding, pressing herself closer with little murmurs of pleasure as his hands roamed over every part of her he could reach until he tore his mouth away from hers, gasping.

"Mirade," he said. "Do you know what you want?"

Her eyes opened and looked into his, as solemn as he had ever seen them. "When my brother returns, I will be betrothed."

He knew, but the words still caught him in the pit of his stomach, leaving him winded. He could only nod.

"I have done my duty to my clan my whole life. Everything I do, I do for them." She slid her hands into his hair, caressing him as she continued to hold his gaze. "Just this once, I want to do something for myself. Just for me."

"I don't know if that will be enough for me," he admitted, and her eyes grew dark.

"It's all I have," she said. "It's everything I have. Please."

Against his better judgment, he allowed her to pull his

mouth back to hers. The passion between them flared fast, with Mirade tugging at the tails of his shirt before he framed her face in his hands and drew slightly away. After a long moment, her eyes fluttered open in puzzlement, and he could not resist dropping another gentle kiss on her lips before he spoke.

"Mirade… sweetheart. If this one night is all we have, I have no intention of spending it in this chair when we have a bed available."

She glanced at him and then over at the bed, as though speaking the words aloud made it real. "What if… what if someone hears us?"

He kissed her again. "You know how to prevent that. I was a very poor teacher if you don't remember."

Her eyes widened. "Oh. Oh, yes, of course."

"And one other thing." He paused for a long moment, then accepted that the question would be awkward no matter what. "Do you know how to prevent conception using your magic? I cannot do it myself, not with these," and he indicated his wrists where the shackles lay.

She gazed down at him for a long moment, then said. "All right."

Mirade stood, and he watched as she cast the spells that would ensure their privacy and her protection. Her hands moved with a confidence they had lacked when their lessons began, her magic flowing out to create a room within the room, one that glowed a shimmering silver like moonlight on the waves outside the window.

He stood and held his hand out to her, and she stepped into his arms for a kiss.

Casting the spell that gave them their privacy lent Mirade an odd sense of calm. This was their night, the only night they would ever have, and Lorien was right. They needed to make the most of it.

As she stepped into his arms, she took a moment to savor everything. The heat of his body radiating towards hers. The slight roughness of his hands as they cupped her face. The glow in his aqua-tinted eyes as he gazed at her, a blue as changeable and shifting as the sea itself. She lifted her face for his kiss and his hands slid away to circle her waist as she pressed herself against him.

His hands stroked up her ribcage and paused. "You're not wearing your stays."

Dazed, she blinked at his words. "I had to get re-dressed by myself after I sent Nurse to bed."

"Naughty girl," he breathed, his mouth only a hair's-breadth from hers. "Are you wearing anything underneath at all?"

"Unlace me and find out," she said, and pulled his mouth back to hers as he laughed.

His clever hands quickly found and loosened the laces at the back of her dress while she pulled his shirt over his head and ran her hands over whatever parts of him she could reach. He slid her loosened dress down her arms and stepped back to let it fall to the floor, his expression controlled as he looked at her standing naked in the glow of her magic.

She tossed her head with an attempt at casualness she did not feel. "Do I look like I did in your dreams?"

He swallowed. "No," he said, his voice rough. "You look better. Beautiful."

After a slight hesitation, she raised her hands to touch him, gliding over his shoulders, his arms, his chest, his belly, his sides. His breath came faster, but he let her explore, his hands clenching at his sides as he watched her touching him.

"You're beautiful, too," she said, and he laughed. With a slight hesitation, he held his arms out, and she stepped into them, pressing herself against him as his mouth came down on hers again. She wrapped her arms around his neck, aware of the sway of her breasts against his hard chest, her soft belly pressing against the ridges of his, his erect cock pressed between their bodies as they kissed, hovering just above the part of her that was beginning to clamor for him.

Before she knew it, he was pulling the bedclothes back and lowering her to the mattress before he stripped off his breeches and followed her down, pressing against her skin-to-skin. The chain attached to the collar around his neck rattled against them, and he impatiently pushed it against the headboard, out of their way. To her surprise, he was shaking a little as he lay his head on her shoulder, his arms pulling her close and then even closer.

"If you try to tell me that you lack experience," she said in a teasing tone, "I fear that I will doubt you."

He raised his head, and what she saw in his eyes made her heart skip a beat. "I do lack *this* experience," he said. "I have never been with someone that I—"

Her hand flew up of its own accord to cover his mouth and stop the word he was about to say. Exultation and sorrow warred within her that they had only realized their own feelings when their time together was nearly over.

"Don't," she said. "Don't say it. It will only make tomorrow harder."

After a long moment, he nodded. She let her hand drop, and then dropped her gaze from his reproachful one. Even though it was her own command, she felt she wronged him by stopping him from speaking because of her own cowardice.

His hands, his beautiful hands, came up to cradle her face and tilt it back up to meet his gaze again.

"If I'm not allowed to say it," he said, "I'll show you instead." And his mouth came down on hers with an aching tenderness that was more arousing than any of their previous kisses, for now they each knew how the other felt even without words.

He kissed her everywhere, with reverence and passion, lingering on her breasts, her belly, her thighs as he worked his way back up. She parted her legs for him eagerly as he lingered, watching her reactions as he toyed with her, first with hands and fingers and then with mouth and tongue, sending her higher until the pleasure shattered her, ripping her apart and renewing her, until he slid up her body, pushed his hands under her bottom, and thrust into her with a groan, filling her as she wrapped herself around him, straining to be even closer as he began to move.

She opened her eyes to see him watching her, and he lowered his head to kiss her.

Her magic surged and swayed around them, as relentless as the sea as their pleasure built together. Faintly, she could feel the echo of his dammed-up magic pressing against hers and she reached out to it, feeling only the slightest brush against the iron. As her arms and legs tightened around him, she peaked again and he surged into her with a shout. For a long moment, she savored the feel of him pressing her into the mattress, their sweat mingling, until he rolled to the side and pulled her to lie across his chest.

As they drowsed together, Lorien reached out to touch one of the loosened coils of Mirade's hair. To the eye, it appeared stiff, but under his fingers it was as soft and delicate as a cloud.

He tugged gently at the curl in his hand, watching as it straightened and then sprang back. Her eyes fluttered open, and she watched him with a most peculiar expression on her face.

"What are you doing?"

"I like your hair." He ran his fingers down another strand, carefully separating it from the others that tried to tangle with it and then letting it go, watching it spring back and fly free before turning his attention to the next one, combing his fingers through her curls to find the ones that tried to form a tangle.

"You don't have to do that," she said, her voice turned a little husky, and he dropped a kiss onto her temple.

"I know," he said, and untangled the next one.

She lay tense against him, her breathing coming fast, and he slid his hand beneath the mass of her hair to cup the back of her head, gently stroking her nape until she rested her head against his shoulder. His other hand continued to move in her hair, separating and freeing the coils from one another. Something about the action soothed him, making him feel he could take care of her in this one small way when everyone else wanted her to take care of them.

Breath by breath, moment by moment, Mirade relaxed against him, her cheek and chin pressing into his shoulder, her breasts and belly melting into his side. His cock began to rise again, but he ignored it, enjoying the intimacy as she allowed herself to cuddle against him, one hand sliding around his ribs as the other caressed his shoulder in a drowsy, absent sort of way.

"I don't want to sleep," she murmured against his skin, and it sent shivers skittering down his spine.

"No?" he said, and nuzzled the top of her head, breathing in the fresh herbal-and-sea scent he would always associate with her.

"No," she said, and raised her head to kiss him as the hand that caressed his side slid downward.

They made love twice more that night, each time more frantic than the first, both of them aware dawn was drawing closer with every moment. At the last, she sprawled on top of him in exhaustion, their damp bodies clinging together.

"I must go," she murmured, and his arms tightened around her.

"I know." He forced himself to loosen his grip so she could slip out of the bed and pull her dress back over her head. He rolled onto his side to watch her.

"You could return me today, you know. Bring me to the parley."

Her hands paused in trying to re-order her tousled hair. "I can't," she said. "Not without my brother here. I cannot surrender the keep without him, and you are the only thing that prevents your father and brother from overrunning us and killing us all."

Lorien had known that would be her answer, but he was still disappointed. "I could stop them."

"Could you?" Mirade's smile was sad as she bent to kiss him, and his hand slipped to the back of her neck to hold her longer when she would have drawn away.

"Be careful," he said, and she smiled at him.

"You're not supposed to say that to your enemy."

"Be careful anyway," he said, and reluctantly allowed her to leave. She slipped through the door like a shadow and he heard the key turn in the lock.

Chapter Eleven

As they rode towards the field where the parley would take place, Mirade did her best to ignore the small discomforts that blossomed as the horse trotted along. It wasn't the animal's fault her thighs ached and her skin prickled where Lorien's night beard had scratched it. The dress she wore was a bit too warm for the day, but she had found a small love bite near the base of her throat while she dressed and switched to a high-necked dress to hide it. She feared everything about her—the way she moved, the way she fell into a daydream before forcing her thoughts away from Lorien—must give her away, but none of those who surrounded her seemed to find her actions strange. No one but Nurse, who had muttered darkly to herself and turned away.

It was only one night, she reminded herself. It could only ever be one night. Even as she rode to this parley, her brother was arranging a marriage with a stranger for her. An alliance to protect her clan.

She could not ignore the needs of her people just so she could dally with Lorien.

Mirade ignored the inner voice which whispered it had been more than a mere dalliance, for both of them.

As Mirade rode forward with the captain of her guard, two figures on horseback waited for her. One was a large, fair man with hair the color of wheat and a beard to match. Beside him was a woman in the garb of a warrior, with a bow and quiver sized for her slight frame slung across her back. A long braid of dark hair snaked over her shoulder, tied at intervals with dyed and beaded leather thongs. The woman returned Mirade's gaze with equal curiosity, and more than a small amount of hostility.

Mirade halted her horse a short distance away and raised her hand in greeting.

"You did not bring him," the man said.

"This was said to be a parley, not a surrender," Mirade said.

The man rumbled something low in his chest, and the woman reached out to squeeze his arm in warning. He continued to glare at Mirade, and she straightened her spine.

"I am Lord Tasgall, Lord Lorien's brother," he announced. He gestured to the woman beside him. "This is Lady Sera, Lorien's—"

"Foster sister," Lady Sera interrupted. "How is he?"

"He is well," Mirade said, flushing a little as her memory flashed a picture of Lorien with his head between her legs. "We have provided him with all due hospitality."

Lady Sera looked Mirade up and down and said, "I'm sure you have."

Looking between the two women with a puzzled frown,

Lord Tasgall broke in before Mirade could respond. "I want my brother freed as soon as possible. To show our good faith, I can pledge that we would only execute those who planned the abduction and leave the rest of your people in peace."

"As I was the one who planned the abduction, my lord, I fear that I cannot accept your offer."

Lord Tasgall's eyebrows rose almost to his hairline. "You? You planned this?"

"Of course," Mirade said. "I would not allow my people to endanger themselves without my direction."

He examined her for a long moment. "You are an unusual woman."

"I am a sorcerer, and the lady of this clan. I do what I must to protect them."

The man glared at her in a way that she supposed made most people's knees knock together in fear, but Mirade did not have the luxury of fear. "What is it you want?"

"An end to the hostilities between our people. Peace, if we can bring it."

"You cannot bring it through abduction!"

"This is the first parley that has been called in over a decade," Mirade pointed out. "At the moment, it seems my goal may be within reach, if we are all sensible and willing to compromise."

Lady Sera's ironic smile held an edge of sadness. "When one is dealing with my foster father, Lady Mirade, words like 'sensible' and 'compromise' rarely enter into the conversation."

Mirade could not prevent herself from smiling back. "Then I'm afraid we will not be able to reach a compromise after all."

"Not today, at least," Lady Sera agreed.

Lord Tasgall glared at each woman in turn before wheeling his horse around to canter back to their lines.

"Good morrow to you, Lady Mirade," Lady Sera said. "I am sorry that we could not reach an agreement."

"I am as well," Mirade said, surprised to find she spoke sincerely. The feud did not mean that there were no good people on the other side. In fact, it only made it more frustrating to know that others wanted an end to the feud but could not find their way.

With one last nod to Lady Sera, Mirade wheeled her own horse and rode away.

As they reached to the edge of the causeway that stretched across to the keep, Mirade felt a hard blow that knocked her from the saddle, the ground rushing up at her as she fell. With a last desperate push of magic, she raised the barrier back in place.

And then she knew no more.

Lorien found he could not settle to anything that day. He told himself it was the sleepless night and tried to rest more, but he continued tossing and turning until, disgruntled, he flung the covers away.

He tried to read, but could not seem to focus on the page.

He paced the length of the room, pausing as he reached each end, but even that could not dissipate his nervous energy.

Something was wrong—he could *feel* it—but the iron that bound him prevented him from seeing what it was.

Just as he was about to begin pounding the walls in frustration, the door opened and two anxious guards peered in at him.

"What is it?"

"You must tend to someone who is injured."

"Why isn't Lady Mirade doing it?"

"She is the one injured."

Lorien started for the door, forgetting about his chains until they pulled him up short. He glared at the senior guard.

"Unchain me. Take me to her."

The man looked torn between two orders. "I am not to let you loose."

"Then unhook the chains and lead me like a dog if you must, but take me to her!"

It was the longest walk of his life, with the guards constantly pulling him back, unable to keep up with him. He had never been out of his chamber without a no-see spell, but he was drawn to her side like a lodestone.

As he charged through the door to her solar, Nurse glared at him, but he only had eyes for Mirade laying limp and still on a low pallet set before the unlit fireplace, her headcloth askew and an arrow buried in her shoulder.

"They shot her in the back," Nurse spat at him, and he crossed to Mirade, tugging impatiently at the chains as he fell to his knees next to the pallet. He smoothed her hair back from her forehead, but she did not stir. Her brown skin held an ashen tone that made his stomach lurch in panic.

"Why did you move her?"

"We had no choice," one guard said, and Lorien shot the man a look that made him step back.

"You could have killed her, you fool." Lorien turned to Nurse. "You must unlock me. I cannot heal her unless you do."

"You must swear not to do her harm."

"Yes, of course, I swear it."

"And if she dies, we will kill you."

He didn't say what he wanted to—that if Mirade died, he would want to die with her—but it seemed his unspoken response was clear, because Nurse said, "Unchain him."

As they removed the last shackle, he felt his magic return in a surge that traveled from his heart all through his spine to his fingers and toes. The others stepped back a pace as sparks ran from his fingers, but he ignored them to lean towards Mirade. He gently touched the shaft that extended from her shoulder and pulled his hand back with a curse.

"Iron," he said. "We must remove it before it poisons her blood, but I cannot touch it and heal her at the same time. Who among you has the steadiest hand?"

He looked around the group, all of whom shrank from him until a woman a few years younger than Mirade took a deep breath and stepped forward. He could see an echo of Nurse in her face and form and knew they must be related.

"I will do it, my lord," she said.

"Very well." He held her gaze with his, willing her to listen. "You must follow my instructions precisely, or she could still die."

"Yes, my lord sorcerer," she whispered, but her gaze did not fall from his, and he nodded shortly.

"Take the shaft in your hand, but do not move it until I

say so. When you do, move it as slowly as possible so that I may heal the wound as the iron moves away."

Lorien took another deep breath to steady himself. He must remain calm, or Mirade could die beneath his touch. He placed his hands on either side of the wound, closing his eyes to better concentrate on what he could sense. The iron of the arrow blocked some of what his magic allowed him to envision, but a small piece of cloth that had stuck to its head showed that the arrow had stopped just short of the closest artery, and he puffed a breath out in relief.

"Now," he said. "Begin. As slowly as you can."

Her face tense, the girl began to draw the arrow out and Lorien sent his magic swirling to follow its path, pushing the piece of cloth up with it so it would not stay inside the wound and cause it to fester.

The slowness of removing the arrow made Lorien want to scream, want to grasp it himself and pull it from Mirade's body in one swift motion, but he knew that could be fatal. The wound was deep and the tissues severely damaged. He tried not to think of how easily she could have bled to death before the troop returned her to the keep. As it was, she lay so still beneath his hands he was afraid she would never move again, her breathing shallow and unsteady.

As the arrow was removed, Lorien's magic followed in its wake, knitting muscle and veins and tissue back together. The blood already spilled within her body could not be replaced, but he knew it would be re-absorbed. If infection did not set in.

It felt as though it took hours. Perhaps it did. Every hitch in her breathing, every twitch of her pain, made him flinch as though it were his own.

Once the arrow was removed and cast aside, he lay with

his head against Mirade's, hands on either side of the wound as he poured healing magic into her until he was dizzy. With agonizing slowness, her erratic breathing steadied, and at last his magic helped ease her into a healing sleep.

Shaking, he got to his feet. "She will live."

As Nurse wept and the rest of Mirade's people crowded around her, Lorien took two steps backwards.

And vanished.

Chapter Twelve

orien ignored the cries of surprise and greeting as he materialized in the center of his father's camp at twilight and strode to the commander's tent. Mud squished between his bare toes—at least, he hoped it was mud—but he ignored the sensation as he threw open the flap of the tent to see his father and brother bent over a table, looking at a map spread out between them. Tasgall was the first to look up, and it lightened Lorien's mood a shade to see the look of joy and relief on his brother's face.

"Lorien! You escaped!"

Tasgall came forward to embrace him roughly. Lorien tolerated it for a moment before he stepped back to nod to his father, Lord Ohrean, who approached more slowly.

"Whose idea was it to shoot Lady Mirade in the back as she rode into her keep?" Lorien said before his father could speak. The older man's brows furrowed together.

"What are you talking about, boy?"

"I spent most of the day fighting to save her life," Lorien

bit out. "If we had killed the lady of the keep, we would have spent the next year trying to besiege it."

"I ordered no such thing," his father insisted, and Lorien looked from one to the other of them.

"Know this," Lorien said. "When I find out who did it, I will have his balls."

His brother stared at him. "She held you captive for over a month."

"I know. I was there, brother."

Lorien lowered himself onto a nearby bench. His knees were still weak from the healing, and from the terror of thinking he wouldn't be able to save Mirade. He lowered his face to his hands and his brother clapped him on the back.

"What you need is food and drink, and clean clothes." His brother frowned at him. "Though they seem to have treated you well enough."

A laugh bubbled up from inside Lorien's chest, a laugh that tried to turn itself into a sob before he caught it. "You could say that."

Duty had required him to escape and return to his own side, but he was no longer certain his duty lay with his father. His loyalties had changed in ways he would need to examine before he could plan his next move in a game whose stakes had risen unbearably high.

Mirade woke in pain, her back and shoulder on fire as she lay on her belly. What had happened?

She turned her head to the other side to see Nurse's youngest daughter Firchara dozing in a chair next to her. At

Mirade's movement, the young woman woke and stared at her.

Mirade tried to clear her throat before she rasped, "Thirsty."

"My lady!" Firchara turned and called over her shoulder. "Mother, my lady is awake."

Nurse bustled to the side of the bed, shaking her head. "Why must you take these foolish actions, Lady Mirade? You nearly got yourself killed."

Despite Nurse's fussing, her hands were gentle as she helped Mirade roll to her uninjured side and held a glass of water to her lips. Mirade drank deeply and let the moisture settle in her throat before she asked the question that was uppermost in her mind.

"Lorien?"

Nurse frowned at her. "In the excitement of your injury, he escaped, my lady, I'm sorry to say."

"Oh." Mirade could not keep useless tears from prickling at the back of her eyes, so she closed them.

"Firchara, give Lady Mirade more water while I fetch her some strengthening broth."

"Yes, Mother," Firchara said, and raised the cup to Mirade's lips again. She drank more, then looked up at the younger woman, who watched her with compassionate eyes.

"How did he escape?"

Firchara paused, then said, "Mother unlocked him so he could heal you. After he did, we all crowded around, and somehow..."

"It's all right," Mirade said. "We knew that he would take the first opportunity he could."

"Let me fetch a cooling cloth to lay on your wound, my

lady," Firchara said. "Mother said you would be sore from the iron, but it should lessen in a day or two."

"All right," Mirade said, and Firchara bustled off on her errand.

She waited until Firchara's footsteps faded from her hearing to let her tears flow free, a storm the like of which Mirade had not experienced since the day her mother had breathed her last and Mirade had realized that saving and preserving her people was a task she must do alone. The wrenching sobs made her wounded shoulder burn with pain, but she could not bring herself to stop until she heard footsteps returning.

She and Lorien had both known they would be on opposite sides again as soon as he was free, but she still felt wretched knowing he was gone from her life. Forever.

There was something familiar nearby.

Lorien's steps slowed as he crossed the Brodhan encampment, and then halted. Soldiers dodged around him as he turned in a slow circle to pinpoint the odd sensation. He was walking to his father's tent, but it was not his father. It was not his brother, who Lorien had left at the evening meal with their men. It was not Sera. It was not even Mirade, leagues distant, but still close to his heart.

As he continued towards the place where his father waited for him, the sensation grew stronger, alien yet strangely familiar, with the signature of an object, not a living being.

Dread rose at the back of his throat, and a whisper of

cowardice urged him to flee back to his own tent and confront his father tomorrow, to give himself more time to absorb this new knowledge and decide what to do about it.

Then his father's lieutenant threw open the flap of the tent, and it was too late to turn back. He ducked his head and entered his father's presence.

"So you finally deign to speak to your liege lord alone, eh?"

Lorien halted before his father's chair and bowed, keeping his expression impassive. The conversation they needed to have would come to an abrupt end if Lorien did not keep a firm hold on his temper. "I thought you would prefer me to wash away the stench of my captivity before we spoke."

"Hmpf." His father looked him up and down. Lorien was back in his own tunic and boots, the extra clothing feeling strange after so many weeks in just a shirt and breeches, but armoring him against his father's criticism. "Tasgall says they treated you well."

"They did."

"And you could not have escaped sooner?"

"No."

His father leaned back in his chair. "Did you at least bring me inside information? Intelligence about the keep we would be able to use?"

"I did learn something very interesting," Lorien said with forced casualness. "Their gramarye was stolen when our feud first began."

"Nonsense. Is that what that woman told you?" His father scoffed, but Lorien watched the tiny tremor of his hands and the quick sideways motion of his eyes instead.

"Yes. That is what she told me."

"And you believed her? The woman who abducted you and held you captive?"

"I did not believe her," Lorien said, and saw tension drop from his father's shoulders. "I argued with her that such an act was far too dishonorable for any Brodhan to commit."

"And you were right to argue that, my boy."

"Was I?" Lorien said. "Or was I misinformed?"

There was a long silence between them, but Lorien knew how to wait.

"You know."

"I know now that the cause of this feud is that we killed their lord and stole their gramarye. And that you have spent the past fifteen years trying to crush them for daring to complain of it. Tell me, Father, if you win—if you kill every man, woman, and child in that keep—will that make his murder right?"

"We must protect our own people!"

"Protect them from what? From facing the consequences of their own actions?" Lorien studied his father's face and sucked in his breath. "You know who did it."

"It was not I."

"No. But you know who it was." The pieces clicked together, forming a new and terrible reality. His father's expression as his own brother's body was carried to him. "It was Doneach. Your brother. Wasn't it?"

There had always been a darkness to his uncle, one that caused Lorien to avoid him even as a child. Among men who drank hard, he drank even harder, and the petty cruelties of his sober state grew into monstrous ones when he was drunk. The fact that he had little magic allowed him to hold the responsibility of handling iron when needed, but he had resented it, and his brother, and whoever else among the Brodhans had magic. Including Lorien.

Only a man with no honor would murder a man and steal another family's gramarye out of spite and jealousy for his own lack of magic, and so one had.

"You see now," his father said, "you see why it had to be this way. You see why I had to protect the family's honor and continue the war until the Mochain clan was crushed."

"I see why you decided that dishonor was the only way to cover up my uncle's crime," Lorien said. "But all you did was take his dishonor on yourself."

"It had to be done," his father insisted. "We could not allow anyone to know… to know…"

"To know that we harbored a murderer and a thief within our own family?"

There was a long silence between them, and Lorien allowed it to hang.

"We could allow no one to know your uncle dishonored our clan," his father said at last.

"And so you made that dishonor worse," Lorien said. "Far worse than it ever needed to be."

He wanted to weep—for Mirade's losses, for the loss of his own boyhood, all for a deadly feud fueled by his father's pride and stubbornness. Instead, he rubbed his forehead, feeling a familiar sense of helplessness when dealing with his father.

"We must return it," Lorien said.

"Impossible. Too much time has passed."

"We must return it, and make restitution."

His father laughed. "I know what's in your mind. Stop thinking with your prick. There will be other women when this one is out of our way."

"Not for me," Lorien said. "Even if you kill her, I will join her clan and protect them from you."

"You would betray me? Betray your home and family?"

"For her? Knowing that she is in the right and you are in the wrong? In a heartbeat."

Imprisonment was no more pleasant when it was his father who had ordered it, but at least he had not been clapped in iron again. Instead, Lorien had given his word of honor not to leave his tent, and his father had stationed four burly guards armed with iron front, back, and sides, to ensure he did not break his word.

He heard raised voices outside and, sure enough, Tasgall soon loomed in the entrance of the tent, glaring down at where Lorien sat with the book he had left behind the morning Mirade had captured him. Sera must have brought it for him, but there was no other sign of her. He had not seen her at all since his return.

"Come in, brother," Lorien said, resigned to his fate, and Tasgall let the flap of the tent fall behind him.

"Have you run mad?" his brother hissed, and Lorien could not stop the wry grin that tugged at him.

"Possibly," he said. "You may as well sit down."

Tasgall fell heavily onto a nearby camp stool, still staring at Lorien. "Whatever possessed you to pledge your loyalty to the Mochains?"

"You will have to ask Father that question," Lorien said evenly. "He knows the answer, and I am honor-bound to not reveal it."

"So it is a matter of honor?"

Lorien looked down at the book in his hands, idly toying with the cover and pages. "Through no fault of mine or yours, the family's honor has been tarnished. Father is the only one who can repair it, but he is too proud to do so."

His brother continued to stare at him as though he no longer recognized him. "You never concerned yourself about such things before."

"I had never seen the results of our dishonor before. Now I have, and I cannot ignore it."

"But you refuse to tell me what Father did that you feel was so dishonorable."

"It *is* dishonorable," Lorien said. "And Father knows it is."

Tasgall was silent for a long moment before saying, "This woman has bewitched you. It is the only answer."

Lorien laughed. "Not in the way you think, brother. I am in full possession of my magic, and she did not use hers against me."

"What about Sera?"

"What about her?"

Tasgall frowned. "How can you marry her when you love another? I have never thought of Sera as anything other than your promised bride."

"I find that most interesting," Lorien said. "Because I have never thought of Sera as anything other than my foster sister, no matter what Father had planned for us. I love her as a sister, and nothing more. To tell the truth, we would be miserable together."

"But Father—"

"I am a man full-grown, Tasgall. As are you. I cannot dance to Father's tune in this, not when I know the truth."

Tasgall shook his head in wonderment, clearly trying to make sense of Lorien's words. "So you will abandon your family and loyalties without a backward glance."

"If I have to." Lorien fixed his brother with a look. "But I would prefer to create an alliance between the Brodhans and the Mochains to bring peace."

"You think we should ally with a clan that has been a thorn in our side for a dozen years?"

"I think we should remove the thorn rather than wage more war, yes. I find myself tired of father's endless feuds."

Tasgall snorted. "What do you expect us to do? Become farmers?"

"Yes," Lorien said. "And trade to the southern seas, as the Mochains were used to do before the feud began. And then we all can be prosperous together rather than spending every waking moment trying to fight each other."

Tasgall sighed and got heavily to his feet. "If you will not see reason, I see no purpose in continuing to speak."

"Ask Sera," Lorien said. "She will know which of us is speaking reason."

"She is too angry with your woman to speak to you, or so she says."

"Is she now?" Lorien said. And wondered.

Chapter Thirteen

L orien moved restlessly through his own dreamscape, waving aside images of his father and his brother, of war and death and siege, as he paced the length of dream-time waiting for the flare of Mirade's magic to reach out to him.

With a suddenness that made even his dream-self a little giddy, he was walking on a rocky beach, waves rolling in and stirring up the pebbles that covered the shore. Mirade was walking towards him, and he held his hands out to her.

"Why are we here?" she asked, but took his hands in hers, tangling their fingers together.

He sighed. "I needed to speak to you, and my father could eavesdrop on other methods. This is safer, for both of us."

Her eyes were sad as she looked up at him. "We must not meet like this. We knew before this began we could never be together."

His hands tightened on hers until he saw her wince and loosened his grip. "I don't believe that."

"Then you are an optimist, my… my friend."

His heart skipped a little at her hesitation—what had she been about to call him instead?—but she continued to speak.

"The most we can hope for is that your father will agree to end the siege and return home and then we… we cannot see each other again."

"No, Mirade." Unable to bear her desolate expression, he gathered her against him, wrapping his arms around her as she leaned her head against his chest. "I have a plan."

He could feel the smile that quirked her mouth. "You always have a plan."

"And sometimes they even work." He dropped a kiss onto the crown of her head.

He had thought their shared dream vivid before, when he was held in iron, but now it was as though they truly stood together in front of the sea, the sharp salt air cutting through his cloak and causing him to draw her even more closely against him to share his warmth with her.

"My father has your gramarye," he said. "He did not steal it, but he knew the man who did, and he has kept it hidden to cover up the crime. I am sorry."

He felt her tremble against him, and did not think it was because of the wind. "I… I had hoped it was not really true."

"So did I," Lorien said, and his arms tightened around her. "But I could sense it when I spoke to him, and when confronted he at last admitted it."

"He'll never return it."

"I don't know." He pulled a little away to look down into her up-tilted face. "If he would return it to you publicly, would that change anything for you? Or for your brother? Perhaps we could end this feud peacefully."

Mirade shook her head. "There have been too many other deaths."

"The feud must end someday, or there will be no one left to fight it. Why not now, with us?"

"I… I have to think. Talk to my brother."

"All right." The edges of the dream wavered. Someone or something was attempting to wake one of them up. "Promise me you will talk to him."

"When he returns. I will try."

He bent his head to kiss her, but she dissolved away from his hands, becoming part of the salt mist that surrounded them.

"Promise me!" he shouted, though he doubted she could still hear him.

Mirade woke with that demand still ringing in her ears, squinting up at Nurse as the older woman crouched over her bed, lamp in hand.

"Are you all right, my lady?" Nurse said anxiously. "You were talking in your sleep."

Tears pricked at Mirade's eyelids, and she turned her head away. "I am fine. I was only dreaming."

Nurse looked skeptical, but said, "Your brother has returned, and was told you were wounded. He wishes to see you."

Mirade sighed. Ronek had always had terrible timing. "Can't he wait until morning?"

"Just a brief visit, my lady. I will not allow him to tire you out."

As was usual, Mirade heard Ronek coming before she saw him, and she groaned softly into her pillow. Of the many things she was unprepared to face, her younger brother was near the top of the list.

As she dragged herself up with Nurse's assistance to lean against the pillows, wincing as her sore shoulder pressed against them, the door to her room slammed open and Lord Ronek of Mochain filled the doorway. He might now tower over her by six inches, with even more height added by the twists of his hair, but he would always be her baby brother in her heart, the boy she had raised since he was twelve summers old to her sixteen. Nurse patted him on the arm as she exited to give them time to talk alone.

He crossed his arms and glared at her. "What have you done this time, Mirade?"

She flinched despite herself. "Only what needed to be done in your absence, brother."

"I was trying to negotiate with Baron Abhra when word of this mad start of yours reached us and caused him to refuse you outright."

"I had no choice," she said sharply. "Sit down so I don't have to crane my neck up at you."

To her surprise, he obeyed, folding himself onto the low chair next to the bed and frowning at her. "Were you badly wounded?"

She shrugged, trying not to wince. "Badly enough. They shot me with an iron-tipped arrow and Lor—my lord sorcerer told Nurse it would take a little time for the poison to work its way out. The wound itself is healing well."

"You held the man prisoner for more than a month and yet he healed you?"

She heard the skepticism in Ronek's voice and scrambled to reassure him. "He is not a wicked man, Ronek. Not at all what he was said to be. He is honorable, and kind, and…"

She trailed off as she saw the look on her brother's face and knew what she had given away. Ronek had always been perceptive, even as a child, as part of his gift of prophecy.

"How big a fool were you, Mirade?"

Tears pricked at the back of her eyes as she dropped her gaze. "Fool enough to fall in love."

Ronek put a reassuring hand on her uninjured shoulder, but they both knew it would not help her pain.

"It does not matter," Mirade said with a bravado she did not feel. "Nurse has told me that the barrier held even through my injury, so there is no need for an alliance. I can protect the keep now."

Ronek gave her an odd look. "I did not only seek an alliance to protect the keep. I thought you might like to be married and have a home of your own."

"This is my home," she said automatically, a moment before a dreadful realization came to her and she looked at her brother. "Unless… unless *you* are planning to wed."

Ronek looked steadily at her. "We could not come to terms," he said. "Not terms that I liked."

"Oh." Relief washed over her as he continued to talk, but melancholy quickly followed it. Of course her brother would wish to marry and continue their family line. And of course any bride he brought to the keep would expect to be mistress of it, not for his elder sister to continue to hold the keys.

She had never thought ahead to the day when her brother

would be full-grown and ready to begin his own family, or what would happen to her when it came time for her to relinquish her position as lady of the keep to her brother's wife.

"And what of this sorcerer you took prisoner, this Lomar?"

"Lorien," she corrected automatically, and flushed a little when Ronek frowned at her.

"The captain of the guard told me what transpired while I was gone," her brother said gravely. "In truth, I would not have thought you would behave so badly when you were holding the man against his will."

Mirade tossed her head and winced as her sore shoulder twinged as if in protest for the lie she was about to speak. "For him, it was merely a flirtation," she said. "He hoped to cozen me into setting him free."

"Is that why the man crouched at your bedside for a full day to try and save you?"

Mirade looked away from her brother's too-perceptive gaze. "That, brother, is none of your business."

Ronek was silent for a long moment. "Were he not a Brodhan, I would thank him for saving your life."

"He would not want your thanks. He didn't... that was not the reason he did it."

"I would thank him anyway."

Lorien had thought being under guard meant he would be left alone, but Sera arrived the next morning as he was finishing his breakfast.

"Good morning, Sera," Lorien said.

"I did it."

"Excuse me?"

His foster sister stiffened her spine and looked him straight in the eye. "I shot Lady Mirade."

"What? Why?"

Sera shrugged. "I was angry. She held you captive for weeks! And clearly had no intention of setting you free, so I…"

A sudden dread seized Lorien's guts. "Sera, you don't… I mean, I know that Father expected us to wed, but *you* didn't… did you?"

"What?" Sera frowned, and then gaped at him. "I didn't —I was not jealous of her!"

"No?"

"No! Well, not in that way."

"Well, in what way, then?"

Sera sighed and turned aside to stare at the canvas wall of the tent. "I don't want you, Lorien, and I know you don't want me. We've only ever been brother and sister to each other. But I… I envied her. She managed to make you love her even though she held you prisoner, when I cannot make the one I love, love me back. He keeps me at his side, we ride into battle together, but it means nothing to him but that I am a good comrade."

She did not have to speak Tasgall's name. They both knew who she meant. Lorien sighed.

"If I could make that happen for you, Sera, you know I would." Lorien stretched his hand out to his sister, and she took it. "Love spells have no staying power."

She shrugged. "I know I cannot force someone to love

me who doesn't feel the same way. I try not to let it make me bitter, but..."

They were silent together for a long moment before Lorien heaved a sigh.

"He's a fool, Sera."

"I know. And I'm a fool for not being able to let go." She squeezed his hand one more time and then dropped it. "I told myself at the time it was a good strategy to try and kill the Mochain sorcerer. But now I know I let my bitterness take the reins when I should not have."

Lorien understood the pain that drove Sera. He could not like what she had done, but he understood it. Even if he could convince his father to allow him to marry Mirade, their people would be as angry as Sera after what Mirade had done. The honor of both clans required more than a mere apology. They would require action.

M irade was able to get up the next morning and resume a few of her duties, with even Nurse satisfied with how quickly she was recovering. Her work had a different flavor today, knowing it was not truly hers, that she was only the caretaker until Ronek married and brought a wife of his own to the keep.

The messenger arrived during the midday meal, the shouts of the guards coming faintly to the hall. Mirade looked up at the same time Ronek did, and when her brother rose from his chair to investigate the fuss, she followed, trailing a few steps behind him, though she longed to push him to a faster pace.

Just outside the barrier, three men in the colors of clan Brodhan stood facing a loose semi-circle of Ronek's men. Each of them wore a white cloth tied around their upper arm—a sign that they had come to speak, not to fight. Still, the scene was tense, with swords and spears held at the ready by the surrounding guardsmen that were only lowered as Ronek and Mirade approached.

"You have come with a message?" he said, and one man stepped forward.

The messenger glanced at Mirade in a way that conveyed more curiosity than hostility, and said, "Are you the Lady Mirade?"

"I am."

"My master, Lord Ohrean, requires you to meet him tomorrow, two hours after dawn."

Ronek barked a short, sharp laugh and Mirade clutched out at his arm before she thought better of it and dropped her hand. "Does your master truly think I would allow my sister to meet him alone? She will have all of our troops at her back if I even allow her to go."

"Ronek," she said, "it is not for you to say whether I will or will not go."

With a grumble, her brother subsided, and Mirade turned her attention back to the messenger.

"To what purpose does your lord summon me in such a peremptory way?"

"He wishes for my lady to account for her treatment of Lord Lorien."

"Lord Lorien left our keep of his own free will," Mirade said coolly. "He can tell you himself that we treated him well during his stay with us. I regret we were forced to keep him as a hostage, but such things are common in war."

"Nevertheless, my lady, Lord Ohrean requires your presence."

Mirade looked at the fuming Ronek, who said, "Tell your lord that we will consider his request. Now begone."

The messenger bowed once to Ronek, then made a lower bow to Mirade before turning with a gesture to his two men and walking back towards the passage through the cliffs. Ronek frowned at their backs and then turned the same frown on Mirade.

"You are not truly considering going to this meeting, are you?"

Mirade sighed. "I don't know that we have much of a choice, brother. I knew that Lorien's… Lord Lorien's father would be angry and demand recompense."

"I don't know why the men listened to you when you proposed such a mad idea."

"They had no choice," she said coolly. "You left me in charge. And Lord Ohrean's troops were only two days' march from being outside our gates until they were forced to turn and search for the lord sorcerer. There was no other option."

"And now you have left us no other option but to answer for what you did."

"I know," Mirade said. But she could not pretend she was sorry.

When she sought Lorien in her dreams that night, he was not there.

Chapter Fourteen

It was foolish and sentimental of her to go to Lorien's room the next morning. Mirade knew that, but could not prevent her steps from turning that way even as her brother and their men awaited her below.

It showed no signs of his presence. The bed they had shared for a single night was stripped, the bare mattress covered to prevent pests and the hangings removed until needed later. It was simply an ordinary chamber again, and her thought that, if she inhaled deeply enough, she could detect his familiar scent, was surely only a fancy.

Her steps took her to stand at the center window, the one where Lorien had preferred to sit or stand to look out at the sea below. Only a tiny sliver was visible, but it sparkled in the morning sun.

A voice from the doorway said, "It's time, my lady."

Tears pricking at her eyes, Mirade started to turn away from the window, back to the door, readying herself for a confrontation with Lorien and his father that could only end with even more senseless death.

A flash of red caught her eye, and for a moment she thought it a premonition brought on by her gloomy thoughts.

She leaned closer to see that, impossibly, a vine had crept up the wall and twined around one of the bars on the window. On the vine was a closed rosebud with red tips just peeking out. Even as she watched, the bud unfurled and a tiny blood-red rose opened into full bloom.

Mirade reached one fingertip out to caress the velvety petals, and it whispered, *I am with you.*

Glancing back at the waiting guard, she saw that he had heard nothing. She reached out and plucked the rose from the vine. Its sweet, delicate scent and the magic it contained washed over her, calming and soothing her.

I am with you, it whispered again, and she knew with whose voice it spoke.

She tucked the rose into the bodice of her gown, careful to ensure that it was secure beneath her stays and resting against her bare skin. The tiny thorns pricked at her, reminding her to stay alert as she rode into danger.

Mirade turned back to the guard.

"I am ready," she said.

They rode to a high plain on the cliffs above the sea, the only open space large enough for the troops of both sides. A ragged path snaked down to the rocky beach below, and Mirade realized with a start that it was the same one where she and Lorien had met in their dream. Faintly, she could hear the roar of the sea as it swirled among the rocks offshore.

Lord Ohrean sat at his ease on his horse, his lieutenant on one side and his son Tasgall on the other. Lorien was nowhere to be seen, though Mirade could feel his presence nearby. She could feel another presence as well—the Mochain gramarye tugged at her as she and Ronek dismounted their horses along with their troop of guards. Tasgall and his father's lieutenant followed suit, but Lord Ohrean remained on his horse.

"It will be single combat today," Lord Ohrean said. "Magic for magic."

Mirade looked up at him, this man she had hated and feared since she was a child. Strangely, she could see signs that reminded her of Lorien, in his face, in his hands. His hair was white and his beard sparse, and Mirade knew this was how Lorien would look when he reached his father's age. If she lived long enough to see it.

"I will accept under only one condition, Lord Ohrean," she said, the prickle of the rose against her skin giving her courage. "No matter how this combat turns out, this will be the end of the feud between the Mochains and the Brodhans. There will be no revenge for the Lord Sorcerer's abduction, no retribution. The feud ends here regardless of who wins."

Lord Ohrean stared down at her for a long time, his gaze unfathomable. At last he nodded. "Agreed."

"Your word of honor?"

His small flinch at her words was unexpected, and he scowled at her. "Yes. My word of honor."

"Then I accept, Lord Ohrean."

"The challenge is accepted!" he bellowed, loud enough

for the waiting crowd to hear it. "Bring forth our champion."

Then, as Mirade had dreaded from the moment he had vanished, the Brodhan forces parted and Lorien strode out from their ranks, his dark green cloak billowing behind him. Despite everything, her heart gave a little leap when she saw him. He had been difficult to resist as her prisoner clad only in a shirt and breeches. In his full regalia of leather and armor and gold plating, he was breathtaking, and she wondered that she had ever dared to take this magnificent man prisoner, much less to fall in love with him.

Ronek caught at her arm as she stepped forward. "Don't do it, Mirade. We can defeat them, or die trying."

"No," she said. "No more death. Lord Ohrean has given his word of honor. If I lose, you must surrender peacefully. Promise me, Ronek."

He gave a reluctant nod and let go of her arm. His gaze turned to Lorien, who had stopped in the center of the meadow. Waiting for her.

Drawing a deep breath, she moved forward across the open space between their forces. Lorien's face as he watched her walk to him was more somber than she'd ever seen it. She stopped ten paces from him and threw back the hood of her cloak, her eyes devouring him. How well he looked in his own clothes, garbed as the nobleman he was, but she missed him as he had been in her tower, her teacher and equal despite his captivity. Now the gulf between them was wider than ever.

"You are well?" he said after a long moment, his deep voice a little gruff. "You have recovered sufficiently for this?"

She bit back the smile that threatened to bloom. "You

are not supposed to ask that. You are supposed to take advantage of my every weakness in order to win."

A tiny smile quirked the corner of his lips in return. "I suppose you are right. Shall we close the circle?"

Mirade nodded, her breath coming fast as she turned and paced the distance away. How was she to fight the man who had taught her most of the magic that she knew? The man she loved?

But it must be done. Her people were depending on her.

As she turned, she saw Lorien's siblings standing nearby —Lord Tasgall and Lady Sera. She couldn't help but return his brother's gaze curiously, and a puzzled look of his own replaced the scowl before he nodded brusquely to her and turned away, Lady Sera's hand on his arm. The other woman looked back for a moment and then quickened her steps to catch back up with Tasgall.

Can you hear me, Mirade?

Startled, Mirade looked around. It was as though Lorien had spoken quietly in her ear, but there was no presence of his body near hers, only the sound of his voice. She looked across the open space to see that he was still a hundred paces distant from her.

Yes, she said inside her own head. *How are you doing this?*

Magic, he replied, and she could see the flash of his smile even across the distance between them.

They are angry with you, he said. *We must give them a show.*

Mirade looked around at the crowd. *Must I be the one to lose?*

Even across the distance between them, she could see his grin flash out. *Do your worst.*

She focused her energy and sent a blast towards him that rocked him back on his heels with its power even as it splashed against the shield he threw up to block it. The crowd surrounding them gasped audibly.

Like that?

In response, he sent a blast towards her, but she countered it, causing their magic to clash and twine together in the middle of the space between them. The two strands twisted and twirled together in a shower of multicolored sparks before dissipating as they ran out of energy.

Mirade gaped at it for a long moment and then glanced across at Lorien, who seemed equally startled.

Has that never happened to you before? she asked, but he only shook his head in a short, sharp negative.

She permitted herself a glance at the spectators. The ones from her side did not seem to notice anything amiss, but Lord Ohrean's face was tight with anger. Hastily, Mirade looked away from him and wound up to send another wave of magic to burst against Lorien's shields, bracing herself for his return.

When it came, it splashed against her shield before it swirled and whirled around her, tugging at her cloak and her curls like a puppy urging her to play with it. Despite the situation, she found herself suppressing a giggle as her own magic responded, swirling just out of reach of Lorien's in a chase that dissipated when the two streams entwined and sank to the ground.

How was she to battle him when their magics refused to cooperate?

L orien had expected a traditional magical duel—the sort of duel he had fought many times before—but his magic was not cooperating.

Her magic was not cooperating.

Or, rather, it was cooperating all too well.

He felt as though he was trying to ride a spirited horse that had made up its mind to go north when Lorien needed to ride south. He could apply the spurs all he liked, but it only caused the horse to fight him harder. Or, even more to the point, like he was trying to hold back a stallion that had scented an interested mare. If he were to ask himself who was the master here, himself or his magic, he feared he would not like the answer.

Lorien supposed it was a useful thing to learn, that he could not use his magic to injure someone he loved. It was a damned inconvenient time to learn it, however, with both of their clans gathered around waiting for one of them to deliver a killing blow.

"Enough!"

Lorien and Mirade both jumped as his father's voice bellowed through the barrier, which dissolved a moment later, allowing Lord Ohrean to stride into the space between them. He immediately whirled on Lorien, pointing an accusing finger at him.

"You thought yourselves so clever, didn't you? Working together to put on a show, a make-believe duel? Well, no more."

Lorien could see Mirade tense, gathering her magic, and he sent her a quick, desperate plea: *Wait.* Slowly, so slowly, her hands unclenched, and he drew a deep breath before returning his attention to his angry father.

"Mirade… Lady Mirade had never seen my magic at full power before, sir. I was in iron while I was at her keep. Neither of us knew that would happen."

"Hmph." Ohrean's eyes bored into his, and Lorien kept his expression as sincere and open as he could. After a long moment, his father waved his hand impatiently.

"None of that matters. You are, both of you, clearly useless against each other in a duel."

"Then we fight," Lorien said bleakly, and Mirade gasped. He reached out to her the only way he could with so much physical distance between them, but his effort slid away and she remained standing straight, glaring at his father.

"You may lay siege to the castle if you wish, my lord," Mirade bit out, "but it would violate the terms of our agreement and your word of honor for you to begin an attack now."

Lorien saw his father's face tighten with anger at Mirade's words. Lord Ohrean raised his voice to be heard as the soldiers of both clans crept forward, glaring mistrustfully at each other from their opposite sides. "A duel can no longer be fought—their magic is too attuned. But I will extend another offer to you, Lady Mirade."

Lord Ohrean turned and faced Mirade fully for the first time. Lorien saw her flinch a little, but only he knew her well enough to see it. Mirade and his father took each other's measure for a long moment, and Lorien felt a surge of pride in Mirade's refusal to be intimidated.

"My son claims that I have something that belongs to your family. A gramarye."

Lorien was unsure if the shock he felt came from himself or from Mirade, for neither of them had expected this turn of events.

"I know you have it," Mirade said after a long moment.

"I know where it is," his father said. "There is a way for you to reclaim it, through a public ordeal. If you survive, I will return your gramarye. If you die, I keep it."

A murmur spread through the crowd. Such public ordeals had been held before, but only rarely, perhaps not even within the lifetime of most of those present. Now they were to watch one happen in person.

Lorien inched closer to her, moving slowly enough that he did not attract his father's attention until he was within arm's reach of Mirade.

"Naturally, I am willing," Mirade said, and her eyes flicked to Lorien's for only a split second. "But the ordeal must take place here, and now."

"Must, girl?" Lorien winced at his father's tone. "To me, you say that I *must*?"

"Yes," she said. "I cannot take the chance that you would attack our keep while I am away east of the sun and west of the moon."

"I would give you my word of honor not to do so."

"Would you?"

Mirade and his father locked eyes for a long moment and then, to Lorien's surprise, his father snorted in amusement.

"Very well. You have your condition, Lady Mirade. Do not think to test me so again."

The tiny rose prickled against her skin as it shifted out of place, and Mirade raised her hand to adjust it, though she was unwilling to look away from Lorien's father. She did not trust his offer but was unwilling to turn it down if it held the promise of the return of the gramarye.

"My son gave you a rose?" Lord Ohrean said, and the note in his voice made her frown at him.

"Yes," she said. Her fingers traced over the petals almost without her conscious thought before she tucked it back out of sight. She pressed her hand against where it lay as it whispered against her skin in that voice that was Lorien's, but that only she could hear. *I am with you.*

"My son has declared his loyalty to you." Lord Ohrean raised his voice so it could be better heard by the crowd. "My question for you, Lady Mirade: does he have your loyalty in return?"

Mirade remained silent, unable to understand the significance of Lord Ohrean's question. She glanced at Lorien, who appeared equally adrift. Their hands floated close to one another, as their magic did, but did not quite dare touch under his father's gaze.

Lord Ohrean gestured, and two of his guards stepped forward. Iron shackles dangled from their hands, designed to block her magic the way she had blocked Lorien's. She felt rather than saw Lorien's protest and his precipitous step forward, but she waved him back, her eyes locked on those of his father.

"This is the ordeal, Lady Mirade," his father said. "Both of you in iron. Both of you unable to use your magic to help the other."

"Father," Lorien said in a tone she had never heard from him before. "If you harm a single hair on her head, you will regret it for the rest of your days."

Lord Ohrean's head whipped towards Lorien, his

surprise unfeigned. "Are you placing a curse on *me*? Here, before my own men?"

"Yes," Lorien said, and his hand moved the rest of the way to Mirade's. She took it. His grasp was warm and reassuring, and he did not look away from his father.

There was a long silence between Lorien and his father, but the older man finally looked away.

"Very well," he said, and gestured the guards forward.

Lorien stepped between them and Mirade and held his hand out peremptorily. "I will do it."

"No tricks," his father said. "She must win honestly."

"No tricks," Lorien said. "But they will not touch my promised wife unless she wills it."

Looking between the two men, the guards handed the shackles to Lorien. He turned to Mirade. She tried not to gape at him, astonished by this public declaration of his intentions in front of their assembled clans.

"I am sorry," he said, and she did her best to smile at him.

"I will do my best to win," she said, and held out her wrists. Carefully, he snapped the fetters around each wrist before kneeling to secure each of her ankles. Finally, with a wince, he placed the last one around her neck, bending to brush his lips against hers before stepping back with a shuttered expression.

It was a most peculiar feeling, having her magic fade away. Like someone had turned down a lamp until there was only the faintest glow at the heart of the wick. Her first thought was that she would need to discuss it with Lorien later, to compare the sensation and see if he had felt the same.

But not now.

Resolutely, she turned to face his father, conscious that Lorien stood at her shoulder, protecting her back from any unexpected strike.

"I am ready," she said.

At another nod from Lord Ohrean, two more soldiers stepped forward with a second set of iron chains. Lorien only shook his head and sighed before presenting his wrists. They stripped his armor away, leaving him in his tunic and breeches, before threading each chain through the shackles and locking them at his feet.

Mirade raised her voice to be heard by the crowd that surrounded them. "You must swear now, my lord Ohrean, before both of our clans, that regardless of what happens, this ordeal will end the feud between us."

"I make no such promise, Lady Mirade."

"Then I will let your son die and continue to fight you," she said, "and you will have gained nothing from today except the murder of your own son."

The older man blanched at that. Lorien's shoulders stiffened, and she wished she could reach out with the mental reassurance she had become accustomed to so quickly, but the iron that chained each of them prevented it. She could only hope that he could read the truth in her eyes as she kept her face impassive.

"Your brother will never agree to such a thing," Lord Ohrean said.

Without looking, Mirade gestured to Ronek, who stepped forward to stand at her other side, glowering at Lorien's father but keeping his hand away from the hilt of his sword.

"If my sister is willing to risk her life to gain peace

between our clans," Ronek ground out, "then I am willing to sacrifice my pride for that peace."

The two men took each other's measure for a long moment before Lord Ohrean grunted. "Very well, Lady Mirade. Lord Ronek. You have my word of honor that this ordeal will end the feud between us. Now let us begin."

At his nod, the guards on either side of Lorien began pulling him down the path towards the beach, to a large rock that his chains could wrap around. He went without a backward glance, his back straight, as the soldiers chained him to the rock and then waded back, the water already surging in with the morning tide. The rest of them trooped behind, Mirade all but treading on Lord Ohrean's heels in her anxiety to reach the beach as quickly as possible.

Lord Ohrean reached into an inner pocket of his tunic and brought out a small book that she recognized even without her magic: the Mochain gramarye, the collected writings of generations of her paternal family's sorcerers. She felt Ronek tense at her side and knew he was tempted to grab it away when it was so very close to being returned, but she placed a hand on his arm to stay him.

"It is a very simple choice, Lady Mirade," Lord Ohrean said, turning so the assembled clans could hear his words clearly. "I can return the gramarye to you now, at this very moment, and you can return to your keep with your men. Or you free my son from his bonds, and I keep the gramarye."

It was a wrench—she could not deny that—but there was only one decision she could make.

"Give me the keys," she said.

Lord Ohrean's head snapped to her. "What?"

"Give. Me. The. Keys."

She knew these tides and knew Ohrean had chosen the worst time of day to challenge them, though she did not know if he was aware of that. Every moment they wasted in speech was another moment that Lorien was at risk.

Ohrean slapped the keys into her hand. She wrapped the chain around her wrist, and plunged into the water, already halfway up her thighs, as she half-ran, half-swam to Lorien.

They could only exchange an agonized look as she ran her hands over his chains. As she had feared, they were attached to his feet, not his hands. Unlocking his wrists would squander valuable time and get them no closer to freeing him. Even as she made her decision, a tall wave descended on them, leaving both of them spluttering, and she knew there was no time to waste.

"Turn your back to the waves," she shouted to him over the crash of the sea.

With a groan, he shuffled the chains around and twisted as best he could. "Give me the keys."

"You can't reach your feet. I can."

She looked down as she groped through the water, but as she had feared, it had already risen too high for her to reach the lock without ducking beneath the waves.

They locked eyes for a moment, then she took a deep breath and dove beneath the churning water.

The waves battered at her, and she fought against them to stay at his feet. Lorien's hands grasped her upper arms, holding her in place as she struggled with the lock that secured his ankles, her fingers going numb in the immense cold of the water. At last, the key clicked, and she pulled at the shank of the lock, but had to struggle back up for another breath of air before it released.

The water had rushed in higher, now swirling around

Lorien's shoulders. There was a tinge of blue to his lips, and his concerned look told her she must look the same. She tried to smile reassuringly while preventing her teeth from chattering.

"It's unlocked. Now I need to untangle us."

She could barely hear herself over the waves. He nodded as though he understood, though his eyes were frantic. She started to take a deep breath, but a wave crashed over both of them, making her sputter and float away. Lorien made a desperate grab. Found a handful of her dress and then her arm, using it to haul her against his chest, his arms tight around her for a long moment before she pulled away and took another deep breath.

The water continued to tug and swirl at her, the current trying to tear them apart, but Lorien's hands were firm under her arms, almost painful, as she released the lock by touch and untangled the chains where they wound around his ankles, fighting the current that tried to knot the chains further until her air ran out and she lunged back to the surface of the water.

The water was to his chin now. Not enough time. Not enough.

She took another deep breath and dove again.

Her hands were numb. Her arms were numb. Her legs were numb. Still she fought through the lack of feeling, trying to keep moving as she tugged at the chains, her lungs burning, unwilling to give up though she knew there wasn't enough time, there wasn't enough time for either of them, she would have to abandon him or die herself.

His hand gripped hers, and she pulled herself up his body, clinging to him as he held her close, his head already under the water.

It was too late.

She wrapped herself around him, lungs burning, steeling herself for the moment when she would have to give up and inhale the icy water, the beginning of the end. His arms held her fast, though she could feel his breath bubbling away, stolen by the freezing water and the relentless drive of the sea.

There was a strange warmth at the center of her chest, and she relaxed into it even as she pushed harder against him.

The feeling grew, reaching out and joining to something else, and she dimly realized it was their magic, reaching out to meet for the last moment as well.

Then the feeling swelled, and the sea receded all around them.

Chapter Fifteen

She raised her head from where it rested against Lorien's chest to look into his startled eyes. There was clear air around them, though she could see the ocean swirling around them, the light inside their bubble a pale green as it filtered through the water.

"What...?"

"I don't know," he said, shaking his wet hair back from his forehead even as his arms remained locked around her. His voice was hoarse, but his arms were strong as they both shivered with cold, sharing what warmth they could. They were dripping wet, she realized, but there was a bubble of energy around them, protecting them from the rushing water. "I think... I think we overcame the iron."

"I didn't know a sorcerer could do that." Her voice was hushed, as rough as his own, and he looked down at her.

"One sorcerer can't," he said. "But it seems perhaps two can, if they're desperate enough."

She looked down to see the chains that had entangled

his ankles lay aside so his feet were free, but her own chains were still in place.

"But how—"

"Sweetheart," he said, "I will be glad to have this discussion when we are no longer underwater."

Mercifully, the keys were still around her wrist, though Lorien had to carefully pull the chain that held them together away from her swollen flesh. Lorien cursed softly as she winced, and she squeezed his hand reassuringly.

"At least I did not lose them in the water," she said, stretching her cramped fingers. He unlocked and removed her wrist shackles, rubbing her wrist until it prickled with sharp feeling as the blood rushed back into her hand, followed closely by her magic. Next, he removed the iron from around her throat, dipping his head to brush his lips against the spot where it had abraded her skin.

Careful not to bump into the wall of their bubble, Lorien stooped down to unfasten the shackles at her ankles and pull the chain away. She sighed with relief as the last of the iron fell away and the rest of her magic returned in a rush. Even as she watched, the bubble around them strengthened and became more opaque, the crash of the surf fading to a dull roar. He handed the keys to her, and she unfastened and unwound his remaining chains in turn.

As soon as his arms were free, he swept her into a close embrace and she leaned her head against his, reveling in his warmth and strength as she wound her arms around his back.

They were *alive*.

But she could only revel for a few brief moments before Lorien lifted his head.

"Now the trick is... how do we return to shore? Or is it better for us to stay where we are until the tide recedes?"

Mirade shook her head, and shivered involuntarily, which only made him draw her closer. "It will be hours before the tide recedes, and we don't know how long we can continue this. We should return to shore."

"Good plan," he said. "How?"

It took some maneuvering to determine how best to move with their bubble, but they were able to use the motion of the waves that cascaded towards the shore to propel themselves.

When they were close enough to the surface to see the light of the sky just above their heads, Lorien halted Mirade with a hand on her arm, and she turned to look at him.

"Can we swim from here? I mean, without the bubble?"

"I suppose we can," she said. "We will end up soaked through again, though. Why?"

He grinned at her, and she returned his look warily. "I would prefer my father to be puzzled as to how we survived."

Mirade decided not to mention the extra push of magic she had felt at that last desperate moment, one that came from an unfamiliar touch.

"All right," she said, and they both took a deep breath before they closed their eyes and let the bubble dissolve around them.

The cold came first, then the pressure of the water as

they kicked to the surface just above their heads, only to be hammered by a wave that hit them from behind.

Lorien came back to the surface sputtering, and Mirade smothered her grin as she swam towards shore. He was close behind her, a clumsier swimmer, but quick to get the hang of using the motion of the waves to propel themselves forward more quickly until at last the rocky shore was beneath their feet.

A lone figure sat on a rock near the shore, wrapped in a heavy cloak. As he stood, Mirade saw it was Ronek, and she staggered through the knee-high waves to embrace him.

"How did you know to wait?"

Ronek shrugged and his dark face colored a little. "Lord Ohrean said you had both survived, but I needed to see for myself."

He drew his cloak from his shoulders and made to drape it around Mirade, but Lorien took it from Ronek and did it himself, rubbing her chilled arms beneath it until she leaned against him. Ronek eyed Lorien with disfavor.

"I suppose you expect to be my brother-in-law now."

"Yes," Lorien said, and Mirade shook her head at the two men bristling at each other.

"I'm freezing," she announced. "Let's go."

Lorien immediately broke the standoff and put an arm around her waist to guide her across the rocky shore. She let him, slanting a glance at her stone-faced brother before leaning further into Lorien's warmth and strength.

They halted at the base of the cliffs, and Ronek looked at her.

"We will go up the other way," Mirade said.

"Will you, now?" Ronek shook his head. "I suppose you do trust him."

"I do." She leaned up and kissed her brother's cheek. "We will see you in the great hall."

Lorien looked between the two of them, puzzled, until she took his hand and led him along the beach to the cliffs beneath the keep. It had been years since she had used the passage, but her magic helped her find the correct spot.

The walk along the beach was familiar from their dream as Mirade halted at a place below the keep where the cliffs were particularly forbidding. She stepped away to set her hands against the rock. The murmur of a spell, the shimmer of her magic, and a doorway opened in the cliff face that had not been there a moment before.

Lorien laughed softly. "No wonder this keep is almost impossible to besiege."

Mirade threw a saucy glance at him before leading him into the passage and re-sealing the door behind them. She cast a small ball of light that led the way up a set of slippery stairs cut into the rock, winding back and forth through the face of the cliff.

Despite her protests that she didn't need his help, Lorien guided Mirade up the stairs with an arm around her waist, which made it all the easier for him to nudge her against the wall and bend his head to kiss her when they reached a sizeable landing between staircases. She turned her head with a giggle and he traced his lips down her neck instead, tasting the salt of the sea drying on her skin, which only reminded him again of the moments when he had thought he would lose her.

"Lorien! We can't." But her stern voice shook a little as he used his tongue on her tender throat. "Your father is waiting for us."

"I don't care," he growled, and pushed his hands under the cloak to cup her bottom and bring her hips hard against his. She gasped and softened a little against him with the yielding that made him a little lightheaded.

"I smell like rotting fish and seaweed." Her voice broke off into a moan and her back arched as he cupped her breast and rubbed his thumb over the peak, bringing her nipple to full attention.

"I still don't care," he said. "I need you, Mirade."

This time, she did not resist when he brought his mouth to hers. The feel of her warm, soft body against his calmed some of the terror of the water closing over their heads at those last moments. He pulled her closer still, his tongue ravishing her mouth until she moaned and arched against him.

Then their magic began to be loosed, sliding from deep within each of them to twine together in its own intimate dance that enhanced how they felt.

He knew he ought to slow down, to be reverent and careful, to show Mirade how much he loved and cherished her as his intended bride, but the agony of nearly losing her was too fresh and sent his hands moving frantically over her, caressing and stroking to reassure himself that she was there, that she was safe, that he had not dreamed their survival.

There would be time for delicacy and care later. Years for it. What he needed now was reassurance that she was alive and unharmed.

His urgency transmitted itself to her, or channeled to her

through their joined magic, because she became as frantic as he, her hands pushing under his clothes to run wild on his salt-streaked skin.

There was nothing on the landing—not a bench carved into the stone, not even so much as a footstool—but it didn't matter. Lorien turned Mirade's back to the wall, hastily ensuring the cloak was between the rough stone and her tender skin before he stripped off her gown and shift while her equally frantic hands pulled off his tunic. The soaked, knotted laces of his breeches frustrated her until, with a gesture, the laces undid themselves almost faster than the eye could follow.

She laughed at his haste, but he swallowed it with another frantic kiss, tongues dancing together as he pressed against her, warming her still-chilled skin with his own until he felt they would catch fire. Her fingers dug into his shoulders as he lifted her thigh to wrap it around his waist.

She pulled her mouth away from his and wrapped her arms around his back, turning her head into the crook of his neck and pulling him close. "I'm all right," she whispered into his ear, and her warm breath on his skin sent a shiver down his spine. "I'm all right. We're alive. I'm all right." Her magic wrapped around him like a silken blanket, soothing his panic but stoking his pleasure.

Her magic calmed him, but only made him more determined. He nudged her chin back up and kissed her again, sweetly this time, and she melted against him as he braced her against the wall. He slid one hand down the inside of her thigh to wrap her other leg around his waist as well, and then up again to stroke her tenderest parts until she moaned and arched against him, tightening her legs around him and reaching down between their bodies to grasp his cock, stroking him until he hissed against her ear.

"Now, Mirade. Please. Now."

She guided him in as he thrust upward, both of them gasping as their magic joined, too, merging and swirling until he could feel her pleasure as his, know how it felt to be inside her and to have himself inside, until his only fear was of losing control.

She cried out and he let himself go, letting their combined magic buoy them until they floated back down again, surprised to feel the ground beneath their feet.

Her beautiful eyes drifted open, and he bent to kiss her.

"I love you, Mirade. We were fated to be together."

She gave him a dazzling smile. "Of course we were. It only took an abduction to prove it."

He laughed and kissed her one last time before, with a grimace, they re-dressed themselves in their still-clammy clothes.

The long, cold trudge up the rest of the stairs and into the great hall of the keep was worth it to see the reaction of the crowd inside as he and Mirade entered through the large doors, Lorien slowing Mirade's steps to make their entrance more dramatic. He could feel her amusement, but she let him lead the way with as much dignity as though she wore her finest gown and not her brother's drenched cloak over her ruined gown.

Tasgall was the first one off the dais, his face alight with a relief that made Lorien feel a little guilty for worrying him so even as he braced himself for his brother's enthusiastic embrace.

"You're alive!"

"Yes, no thanks to Father," Lorien said, but glanced his

father's way. He did not look quite as surprised as Lorien had hoped behind his facade of icy calm, and Lorien wondered again exactly how their magic had overcome the iron at the most crucial moment.

To Lorien's surprise, his brother reached out a long arm and enfolded Mirade in the embrace as well. She gasped, but then laughed and returned it as best she could.

The crowd around them parted as Lord Ohrean stepped down from the dais and Lorien and Mirade turned to face him. Her hand reached out to Lorien's from beneath the cloak, and he twined his fingers with hers as they watched his father approach and stand before them for a long moment.

"I am not familiar with the sea," Lord Ohrean said at last. "The elements were stronger than I had thought they would be. I... I did not expect the ordeal to be as difficult as it was."

Mirade looked between him and Lorien.

"And...?" Lorien prompted his father.

Lord Ohrean gusted out a long breath. "And I am... I am..." His voice faded and then came back more strongly. "I am sorry."

His hand went to his tunic once again. "This is yours, Lady Mirade. You have earned it, and my son's life. Treat them both with care."

Mirade took the book, and Lorien could feel a tiny surge of power from the gramarye course between them. She curtsied to his father as best she could with one hand in Lorien's and the other holding the book, showing Lord Ohrean the deference of a daughter.

"My thanks, Lord Ohrean. I will."

Nurse bustled forward. "We must get you into a hot bath

at once, Lady Mirade, lest you catch a chill." The older woman looked Lorien up and down for a long moment, and he grinned at her. "You as well, my lord sorcerer. Both of you, upstairs."

Lorien held up his hand, and Nurse stepped back with a new deference towards him. He turned to face the crowded hall, and his hand slipped from Mirade's to curve around her waist. She looked up at him as he spoke, her face glowing with the same happiness he felt.

"There are still contracts to sign and rituals to enact," Lorien said, "but as of this day, the Lady Mirade is my wife. Any man who wishes to dispute that may try his luck against me… if he dares."

Epilogue

Lorien looked around the tiny room, a bit disconcerted by the fact that all the furniture was bolted to the floor, but the lapping waves were now a comforting and familiar sound.

"How do you like it?"

He turned and held his hand out for Mirade—his bride, his wife of nearly six months—as she came through the door of the cabin. The miracle of it all still astonished him as he pulled her close and kissed her.

"Are we both going to fit in that bed?" He nodded to the frame and mattress in the corner, piled high with silken pillows, and she laughed.

"It's called a bunk, my love. And, yes, we will fit quite nicely, as long as you don't mind being pressed close together all night."

"I never mind that."

She snuggled against him as he braced his legs against the rocking of the ship. It had taken months of preparation, but at last their voyage to the southern seas was nearly underway. His father had frowned and muttered at the amount of gold Mirade had insisted was necessary to outfit the ships and bring back goods, but had given it in the end with their promise to return it threefold.

Lorien had been more captivated by his wife with each passing day as she went about the business of the preparations, helping where he could, supporting her as he watched her turn her dreams into reality. Now the day had arrived and their ships were ready to sail, with he and Mirade leading the voyage.

"Will we be able to find your mother's family after all this time apart?"

"I think so." She slanted a roguish glance up at him. "My grandfather was reluctant to let his daughter run off with a mere lordling from a distant land when she could have married the son of another successful merchant, but she eventually prevailed. He will be interested to see that his granddaughter went to even further extremes to find her own husband."

"I look forward to meeting them. I look forward to the whole adventure."

Receive a special bonus epilogue for Impossible Tasks *by signing up for Alexa's newsletter*
https://dl.bookfunnel.com/cg628f5gy2

Acknowledgments

I had invaluable assistance from three people for this story: Jen Graybeal, a lifesaver who helped me talk it through with her editor's eye; Whitney Jones at Empowered Writing, who did the developmental edit; and my lovely and talented author friend Caro Kinkead, who did the final beta read to find the rest of the places it needed to be tightened up. I am also grateful to The New Romance Café, the original publishers of this novella, especially Jenny Simon and Andie Wood, who listened to all of my angst as I wrestled with the story.

Tom Hiddleston and Zawe Ashton were my muses for these particular characters, but the real inspiration to tell love stories comes from my husband, who never falters in encouraging me to chase my dreams.

About the Author

Alexa Santi loves storytelling of all kinds, so it's no wonder it took some time for her to settle on fiction after several detours that included an MFA in Screenwriting from Loyola Marymount University. She lives near Los Angeles with her sexy archivist husband and their pesky cats, who insist that she take frequent breaks from her writing to pay attention to them. You can find her on Facebook, Instagram, or on her website at https://www.alexasanti.com/

www.ingramcontent.com/pod-product-compliance
Lightning Source LLC
Chambersburg PA
CBHW031409310726

48971CB00003B/796

9 798989 618200